Bhagavad Gita

Bhagavad Gita

A New Verse Translation by Stanley Lombardo

Introduction and Afterword by Richard H. Davis

Hackett Publishing Company, Inc.
Indianapolis/Cambridge

22 21 20 19   1 2 3 4 5 6 7

For further information, please address
   Hackett Publishing Company, Inc.
   P.O. Box 44937
   Indianapolis, Indiana 46244-0937

   www.hackettpublishing.com

Cover design by Brian Rak and Elizabeth L. Wilson
Interior design by Elizabeth L. Wilson
Composition by Aptara, Inc.

Library of Congress Cataloging-in-Publication Data

Names: Lombardo, Stanley, 1943– translator. | Davis, Richard H.,
   1951–author of introduction, author of afterword.
Title: Bhagavad Gita / translated by Stanley Lombardo ; introduction and
   afterword by Richard H. Davis.
Other titles: Bhagavadgåitåa. English.
Description: Indianapolis, Indiana : Hackett Publishing Company, Inc.,
   [2019] | Includes bibliographical references and index. | In English,
   translated from Sanskrit.
Identifiers: LCCN 2018042396 | ISBN 9781624667893 (cloth) |
   ISBN 9781624667886 (paper)
Classification: LCC BL1138.62 .E5 2019 | DDC 294.5/92404521—dc23
LC record available at https://lccn.loc.gov/2018042396

CONTENTS

INTRODUCTION

The *Bhagavad Gita* opens with one of the most compelling scenes in Indian, or world, literature. Two enormous armies have been drawn up opposite one another on the expansive plain of Kurukshetra, the "field of the Kurus," in northwest India. Both are vast and fearsome and both seem impossible to withstand. Teeming with elephants, chariots, and horses, they resemble two opposing forest ranges. One side is allied with the five Pandava brothers, the other with their cousins, the one hundred Kaurava brothers. The great elderly warrior Bhishma, surrogate grandfather to both sides, lets out a resounding battle cry like a roar of a lion and blows his conch shell. Leading warriors on both sides answer his call with their own blasts on conches. Throughout the two armies the tumult of cymbals, kettledrums, horns, and conches rises to a crescendo, reverberating fearfully across the sky and earth. And into the no-man's-land between the two armies ventures one chariot. The most potent warrior on the Pandava side, Arjuna, has asked his charioteer Krishna to drive him there so he can survey the two opposing forces.

When the warrior and charioteer arrive there, however, Arjuna's zeal for the coming battle begins to wane. He is overcome by pity, and he feels like he is falling apart. As he reports to Krishna,

> Seeing my own people, Krishna,
> drawing near in battle frenzy,
>
> Both my legs collapse beneath me,
> my mouth is dry, my tongue is cracked,
> all my body shakes and trembles,
> my hair bristles and stands on end.
>
> My bow Gandiva falls from my hand,
> and my skin feels like it's burning.
> I cannot stand in position,
> and my mind is wandering off. (1.28–30)

Arjuna explains that he can see no good that could possibly result from the coming war. He views it as a terrible sin. Finally, with his heart overwhelmed by grief, Arjuna sits down in the rear of the chariot and drops his bows and arrows.

This is surprising indeed. Throughout his life Arjuna has been the most fervent and accomplished of warriors. As a member of the ruling Kshatriya class, he has been trained by the best teachers available in the arts of war. In contests among his peers he has consistently prevailed. Moreover, in preparation for this long-anticipated battle with the Kauravas, Arjuna has undertaken a lengthy and arduous journey to collect weapons. He performed rigorous austerities in the Himalayas, wrestled with the god Shiva, and visited Indra's heaven. Now he comes to the battlefield armed with an array of weapons of truly mass destruction, including the fearsome Pashupata weapon that is capable of burning up the entire world. No one would expect Arjuna, of all warriors, to suffer from battle fright.

But it may not be so surprising after all. Battle may be the métier of a Kshatriya male like Arjuna, but war also represents a failure. In this case, the vast hordes of warriors have gathered at Kurukshetra because one family has failed to resolve its own differences. The *Bhagavad Gita* is a portion of a much longer epic poem, the *Mahabharata*, which tells in detail how the Kshatriya lineage descending from the great king Bharata has fallen into deep and irreconcilable conflict. The closely related Pandava and Kaurava brothers are at each others' throats over a throne. When Arjuna speaks of "my own people," he refers to his own first cousins, the Kauravas, as well as other close relatives. Arjuna recognizes this internecine hostility to be evil.

> Do we not know enough, Krishna,
> to turn aside from such evil?
> To understand how wrong it is
> to destroy friends and family?
>
> With destruction of the family
> ancient family customs vanish,
> and lawlessness overpowers
> the entire family structure . . .
>
> Men whose family laws are wiped out
> dwell in hell indefinitely.

Have we not heard this repeated,
again and again, Lord Krishna? (1.39–40, 44)

Destroying the family, corrupting society, creating chaos, dwelling in hell—
to Arjuna the stakes appear high indeed.

Krishna's first response to Arjuna's trauma, naturally enough, is astonishment and scorn.

Why has this craven timidity
appeared at this critical hour?
It is ignoble, Arjuna,
and closes the gates of heaven.

Son of Pritha, do not give in.
This cowardice is beneath you!
Shake off this vile faint-heartedness
and rise up, O Scourge of the Foe! (2.2–3)

Sounding like the coach of a football team trailing at halftime, Krishna berates Arjuna's lack of resolve and rallies him to action. In the culture of the Kshatriya class, with its ethos of honor and heroic manliness, Krishna's allusion to emasculation (*klaibyam*, impotence) is a particularly low blow. However, Arjuna does not give in to Krishna's scolding, not right away, for his qualms about this war are much more profound. And it is thanks to the depth of Arjuna's concerns that we have the seven hundred verses that constitute the dialogue of Arjuna and Krishna that make up the *Bhagavad Gita*. All action is suspended as warrior and charioteer begin a discussion that moves from battle anxiety to ethics, theology, and a vision of God. Krishna pulls out all the stops in his effort to overcome Arjuna's doubts and to persuade him to fight.

Teachings on the Field of Battle

Krishna shifts quickly from his first attempt to shame Arjuna. Faced with a fearsome battle of uncertain moral status, Arjuna will require stronger reasons to fight. Krishna begins to develop a more compelling and persuasive argument. To do so, Krishna draws on many ideas and practices that would have been familiar to a well-educated member of the ruling class in classical India, as Arjuna was. He also introduces several new and truly innovative concepts, and synthesizes them all into his compelling case. It is not possible to summarize Krishna's full presentation here, but it is worth following the conversation to highlight some of the key ways Krishna addresses Arjuna's deep reluctance on the field of Kurukshetra.

Arjuna has good reasons for his trepidation. He is filled with grief for the terrible violence and death sure to result from the battle. And he is also confused. Surveying the enemy ranks, Arjuna sees his cousins, uncles, nephews, grandfathers, friends, and revered teachers. This is a family conflict. It is certainly a principle of good conduct that one does not kill one's own kinsmen. Yet Arjuna is a Kshatriya, a trained member of the warrior class, whose duty is to fight in a just war. What exactly is his responsibility here? Arjuna summarizes his plea to Krishna directly:

> I am overwhelmed with a sense of pity,
>   and my mind is confused as to my duty.
> What would be best, I ask You? Tell me clearly.
>   Advise me, Your disciple, I beseech You. (2.7)

Krishna must first counter both Arjuna's psychological state of anticipatory remorse and his moral confusion as to his proper duty or *dharma*.

Krishna first speaks to the grief. "You mourn those who should not be mourned," he begins, and goes on to assert that persons who "truly are wise" do not mourn either the living or the dead (2.11). Naturally this raises a question: why don't they? Isn't it normal for humans to grieve over the dead? Krishna tells Arjuna that, in fact, all these warriors he is facing on the field of battle will not cease to exist. Here he draws on a premise that all the truly wise in classical India had come to share. With few exceptions, all religious philosophies in India at that time accepted some notion of transmigration, the continuing existence of a person's essence—the soul or spirit or Self— before birth and after death. Krishna uses the catch-all term *dehin*, literally "that which possesses a body" (or "embodied being" here), to designate this transmigrating essence. If one accepts this idea, it leads to a radical redefinition of death. Moving from one body to another is like taking off old clothes and putting on new ones. And likewise, it throws into question any simple notion of killing.

> One who knows the indestructible,
> the eternal, undying, unborn—
> how can he cause one to be slain?
> Whom, Son of Pritha, does he slay? (2.21)

The answer to Krishna's rhetorical question is that a warrior like Arjuna can only slay the bodies of his opponents, while their indestructible and undying souls will remain. So, Krishna tells him, "you are obliged not to lament" (2.25).

This rethinking of death may help alleviate Arjuna's emotional distress, but Krishna must also answer his ethical dilemma. Arjuna is caught between his class duty as a Kshatriya warrior and his family responsibility as a member of the extended Bharata clan. This is not a question of the metaphysics of the soul but of moral judgment concerning *dharma*. Krishna responds to this quandary with decisive aplomb.

> Perceiving your own proper duty,
> you should not tremble or waver.
> Nothing is nobler than rightful war
> for those in the warrior class. (2.31)

In the ranking of moral considerations, Arjuna's responsibility as a Kshatriya warrior to engage in a just war outweighs the obligation he owes to his own kinsmen. Failure to fight, Krishna adds, would be to give up honor and to incur personal guilt. He promises Arjuna that joining the battle will not lead him to a bad end.

But this raises a new question, even if Arjuna does not articulate it here. Combat is a form of goal-directed action. One goes to war, as Arjuna has previously observed, to achieve goals like victory, royal pleasures, kingship, and luxury. Many of the truly wise religious philosophers of classical India—Buddhist and Jain ones as well as orthodox Brahmins—had identified desire and greed as a core human problem. They argued that action based on desire leads inevitably to bondage. The way to avoid this bondage, therefore, was to renounce all desire-based actions. The best method for doing this, they believed, was to leave one's position in family and society, to abandon one's worldly actions, and to live as a mendicant. Through renunciation one might gain release or liberation from all bondage. Arjuna has already proposed something of this sort: "Better to beg alms in this world than to kill my honored teachers" (2.5). Krishna feels he must reconcile his advocacy of worldly action with the spiritual claims of the renouncers, by speaking now of "*Yoga*."

Krishna admits that most human action is indeed motivated by desires and directed toward goals. Even those Brahmin priests, with their flowery hymns and their complicated Vedic sacrifices, are greedily seeking heaven, pleasure, and power. But there is another way of acting, he goes on, that does not fall into the trap of desire.

> Your only right is to action,
> never to the fruits of action.
> Never give rise to this motive,
> but don't be inactive either.
>
> Do all things steadfast in *Yoga*,
> without attachment, Arjuna,
> the same in failure and success.
> *Yoga* is equanimity. (2.47–48)[1]

In effect, Krishna is proposing a new form of renunciation. Arjuna does not need to abandon action, but rather he should renounce his attachment to the fruits of his actions. More significant than the action itself is the impartial, disciplined state of mind with which one carries out the action. The mental discipline, or *Yoga*, of equanimity cuts away the bondage of action, even while engaging in action. And this, says Krishna, is what the truly wise have done.

> The truly wise, minds enlightened,
> who have abandoned action's fruits,
> are freed from rebirth's bondage
> and go to where there is no pain. (2.51)

No doubt this mental discipline is easier said than achieved. Without disputing Krishna's novel theory of action, Arjuna asks for some elaboration. Doesn't this way of acting require a rather special kind of person? To engage in worldly actions—especially on a turbulent battlefield—with the kind of equanimity Krishna recommends, one would have to be a *sthitaprajna*, an

---

1. For glosses of terms italicized in the translation, see the Glossary and Index of Sanskrit Names and Terms.

extraordinary person in whom "wisdom stands firm." Could Krishna please describe such a person?

In classical India, many groups of religious seekers had experimented with physical and mental techniques to gain mastery over the body, the senses, and the mind. The most general term for these practices of self-control is *Yoga*. This Sanskrit term is much broader, certainly, than the word "yoga" as it has been adopted into modern English. From the same Indo-European root as the English word "yoke," *Yoga* can denote the harness by which Arjuna has hitched four horses to his chariot. It can point to any strenuous activity that requires an exercise of will. In the *Mahabharata* the warriors yoke themselves to battle. For the renunciatory groups, *Yoga* refers to all sorts of challenging disciplinary practices aimed at gaining self-mastery. Ultimately, they believed, the disciplines of *Yoga* would lead to an autonomous self-perfection and to liberation from all suffering and from the cycle of transmigration. Patanjali codified many of these techniques in his *Yogasutras*. And throughout the dialogue of the *Bhagavad Gita*, Krishna offers an extended explication of several forms of *Yoga*.

Here Krishna suggests that the techniques of the renouncers offer a method to achieve the mental equilibrium that allows detached action. This begins with the *yogic* technique of withdrawing the senses, "like a tortoise withdrawing back into its shell" (2.58). For one who seeks to become a person whose wisdom stands firm, the senses are the most immediate threat. They lead to attachment, desire, anger, delusion, and finally to the extinction of all wisdom, "a ship blown by wind on water" (2.67). One who gains control over the senses and accepts their impressions with neither attraction nor aversion attains serenity, just as the ocean accepts all the rivers that empty into it. This is the starting point of *Yoga*, and it leads finally to peace.

> The person who casts off desires,
> who acts free from craving and lust,
> indifferent to "I, my, me,"
> that person will arrive at peace. (2.71)

The peace to which the religious renouncers aspire is also available to those who remain and act in the world, Krishna claims, provided they act with the proper mental state of equanimity.

But this does not entirely answer Arjuna's dilemma. If Krishna claims that the attitude of mind with which an action is undertaken is more important than the action itself, why does he urge Arjuna to engage in the "awful action" of war? Krishna may have given Arjuna a way to act, but not a means to evaluate which action, if any, to select. So Arjuna asks for a clarification.

> Your words have a double meaning
> and confuse my understanding.
> Tell me this, and tell me clearly,
> how to attain the highest good. (3.2)

Arjuna's concern with attaining the "highest good" here looks beyond the battlefield of Kurukshetra to the broader field of moral and religious battle in classical India. This was a period of intense debate over fundamental questions, with many teachers and schools each claiming to offer superior means to reach the highest good.

Krishna responds by outlining many of the systems of thought and practice, and by giving his own evaluation of their efficacy. Later commentators have conveniently classified them into three disciplinary methods or paths: the *Yoga* of Action (*karma-yoga*), the *Yoga* of Knowledge (*jnana-yoga*), and the *Yoga* of Devotion (*bhakti-yoga*). The first two of these would have been familiar to an educated Kshatriya like Arjuna. The discipline of action includes the rituals of sacrifice, which had been so prominent in the Vedas. But it also encompasses the responsible performance of one's social or class-based duties, or *dharma*, such as Arjuna's duty as a Kshatriya to fight in this just war. *Jnana Yoga* refers to those systems of philosophical analysis that lead to the highest, most penetrating form of comprehension. Among these systems, Krishna pays much attention to the dualist Samkhya school of phenomenological analysis and to the Vedanta metaphysical speculations first articulated in the Upanishads.

In general Krishna endorses these existing disciplines. He accepts a plurality of paths, viewpoints, and methods as valuable to spiritual ends. But the underlying reason for their efficacy, he argues, may not always be what their practitioners imagine. Take Vedic sacrifice as an example of *Karma Yoga*. Krishna has previously condemned the Vedic priests and their sponsors who perform sacrificial rituals to gain specific goals:

> Greedily intent on heaven,
> seeking rebirth as *karmic* fruit,

they perform abundant rituals
aimed at pleasure and at power. (2.43)

Not all sacrifices are so avaricious, however. Like any action, sacrifice can be undertaken in a mental state of attachment or in one of detachment. Krishna praises the latter.

Mind indifferent, self restrained,
renouncing all acquisition,
acting only with the body,
one incurs no guilt in action. (4.21)

Attachment gone, liberated,
mind grounded deep in knowledge,
performing work as sacrifice,
one's *karma* wholly melts away. (4.23)

Krishna's new theory of action allows him to identify a "good sacrifice" not in terms of any particular action but rather in terms of the state of mind of the performer.

Similarly, the disciplinary practices of knowledge or *Jnana Yoga* can offer great benefits to one who seeks the highest end. For example, the Samkhya school stresses a phenomenological analysis of human experience, grounded in a fundamental duality. The soul or spirit (*purusha*) is ultimately independent from the psychological activities of the senses and the mind. This discriminating awareness can lead to detachment of the "I" in the midst of action.

"I do not do anything." Thus
thinks the *yogin* who knows the truth,
seeing, hearing, touching, smelling,
eating, walking, sleeping, breathing,

Talking, excreting, taking hold,
eyes opening and eyes shutting,
certain that the senses abide
in the objects of the senses. (5.8–9)

One acts in myriad ways, but the innermost spirit does not in fact engage in this action. Likewise, the understanding of a universal, underlying Brahman, as set forth in the monistic Upanishads, can have great value in leading to equanimity.

> Not rejoicing at the desired
> nor grieving at the undesired,
> with mind firm and undeluded,
> knowing *Brahman*, firm in *Brahman*.

> Without clinging to sensations,
> finding happiness in the Self,
> through *Yoga* at one with *Brahman*,
> one attains lasting happiness. (5.20–21)

In this Vedanta-based vision, the innermost Self is understood to be "at one" with the underlying essence of the cosmos, known as the *Brahman*. Whether one adheres to the dualistic metaphysics of the Samkhya school or the monism of the Upanishads, the crucial matter for Krishna is not which one is philosophically correct. Rather, he endorses either school insofar as its discipline of knowledge leads one to a state of equanimity or mental detachment from the fruits of action. Through this equanimity comes lasting happiness.

At the conclusion of his discussion of the discipline of knowledge, Krishna adds one final sentence that neither the adherents of Samkhya nor those of Vedanta would have readily accepted.

> By knowing Me, the Enjoyer
> of sacrificial austerity,
> the world's great Lord, the Companion
> of all beings, he comes to peace. (5.29)

Here is an entry to the third path, the discipline of devotion or *bhakti*. To make sense of this new form of discipline, we must first consider the "Me" of this verse: Krishna the human charioteer who is also "the world's great Lord."

In the *Mahabharata*, Krishna is a Kshatriya prince, like Arjuna. He is the leader of the Vrishni clan, and he rules a kingdom in distant Dvaraka on the Gujarat coast. He is cousin to the Pandavas, since his father Vasudeva is the brother of Kunti, mother of the three oldest Pandavas. He also becomes Arjuna's brother-in-law when he encourages Arjuna to abduct and marry his own sister Subhadra as a second wife. Krishna forms a close friendship with Arjuna and the other Pandavas and often acts as their advisor. And at

Kurukshetra he acts as Arjuna's charioteer, a weaponless noncombatant who is nevertheless extremely close to the action.

As their dialogue on the battlefield continues, however, Krishna begins to reveal another side to his identity. He is a god, a divine "Companion of all beings," who comes into being through his own volition. He does so, he explains, to support *dharma*.

> Whenever *dharma*, or righteousness,
> decreases, O Bharata,
> and unrighteousness increases,
> that is when I create Myself.
>
> For protection of the righteous
> and destruction of evildoers,
> for establishment of *dharma*
> I come to be from age to age. (4.7–8)

The divine Krishna comes into being, or "crosses down" (*avatara*) into physical form, intentionally, to intervene in human affairs for the benefit of the righteous. This puts a whole new spin on the dialogue between charioteer and warrior.

In the world of the *Mahabharata*, a multitude of divine figures populates the heavens and the earth. Many deities exercise superhuman powers in their various spheres and enjoy the patronage and honor of human votaries within this polytheistic setting. Arjuna himself has encountered many of these gods prior to the battle. In fact, he is the son of one of them, Indra, just as his brothers are the half-divine offspring of other divine fathers. Arjuna had assisted the fire god Agni in burning the Khandava Forest, received weapons from several deities, and wrestled with the great god Shiva to acquire the most formidable weapon of them all, the Pashupata weapon. He even spent five years living with his father Indra at that god's heavenly court. But now, his charioteer advances an audacious theological self-portrait that goes beyond any of the gods Arjuna has known.

> There is nothing higher than Me,
> O Arjuna, Wealth's Conqueror.
> All that exists is strung on Me
> like pearls and jewels on a thread. (7.7)

Krishna is the connecting thread of all existence. Further, he claims to be the source of all the other gods, while remaining a step beyond their comprehension.

> Neither the multitudes of gods
> nor the great seers know My origin.
> I am the universal source
> of all the great seers and the gods. (10.2)

Yet here he is, too, in the form of a human Kshatriya prince, a friend and advisor to Arjuna. Krishna is both a transcendent being who encompasses and surpasses all other gods and also an immanent deity who takes an interest and intervenes in human affairs.

The *Yoga* of Devotion denotes an attitude of loyalty toward, adoration of, and participation in a personal divinity. As Krishna presents it to Arjuna, the *Yoga* is not so much a specific disciplinary action but rather a mode or state of mind within which one can engage in other activities. One may perform a sacrifice, a form of *Karma Yoga*, but do so in a devotional spirit. The important thing is that the sacrificer recognizes fully that Krishna permeates every element and movement of the sacrifice. Krishna explains:

> I am the rite and sacrifice,
> the offering, the healing herb;
> I am the sacred text, the ghee,
> the fire and the poured oblation. (9.16)

With this understanding in mind, one transforms the sacrifice into an act of devotion to God Krishna. It is not the act itself that is important but the mentality of the actor. One need not have all the wealth required to offer an elaborate public sacrifice. Krishna equally accepts humble offerings, provided they are given in the proper spirit of devotion.

> A leaf, a flower, fruit, water
> offered to Me with devotion
> by anyone whose heart is pure
> is an offering I accept.
>
> Whatever you do, whatever you eat,
> whatever sacrifice you make,

all of that, O Son of Kunti,
do as an offering to Me. (9.26–27)

By "anyone," Krishna goes on, he means all those—"women, merchants,
even outcastes"—who take refuge in Him will attain the highest goal. Unlike
Vedic sacrifice, this path of devotion is open to all.

Krishna explains his own divine nature as the Supreme Being at consider-
able length. In the end, Arjuna pronounces himself convinced: "I believe that
all You tell me is the truth, O Handsome-haired One" (10.14). It has cleared
up his delusion. But he would like just one last confirmation. Krishna has
described Himself in words. Arjuna would like a visual proof.

Just as You have described Your Self,
I would like, O highest Lord,
to look upon Your godly form,
O Spirit unsurpassable.

If You think it is possible
for me to see You like this, Lord,
then make Your everlasting Self
visible to me, God of *Yoga*. (11.3–4)

Krishna immediately responds to his friend's earnest request. What follows is
an extraordinary vision, in which Arjuna is able to see Krishna's "everlasting
Self" in all its glory.

At first Arjuna's vision confirms what Krishna has just said of himself. He
sees all the other gods contained within Krishna's inclusive being. He sees the
entire universe in all its diversity assembled in that one divine body. Krishna's
body radiates dazzling light, more than even a thousand suns. But as Arjuna
gazes with the divine eyesight Krishna has granted him, he begins to get
alarmed. He loses his nerve.

Having seen all Your mouths with their many tusks,
    blazing like the fires that destroy time and space,
I don't know which way is which, I find no comfort.
    Have mercy, Lord of Gods, Abode of the World! (11.25)

The Supreme Being appears to Arjuna like the fiery conflagration that brings
about the destruction of the world. This is entirely pertinent to Arjuna's

own situation, facing an imminent battle of gruesome proportions. Arjuna now sees both his enemies and his allies, all disappearing into Krishna's open mouths, like moths flying into a flame.

This is baffling to Arjuna. He has already made the leap in recognizing his friendly cousin as God. But didn't Krishna state that he had appeared in order to support *dharma*? Didn't he say he was a friend of all beings? What is he doing at the center of this slaughter? Arjuna prays for mercy and asks for an explanation.

From his Supreme Form, Krishna speaks:

> I am Time, mighty world-destroyer,
> come to annihilate every world. (11.32)

As Supreme Being, Krishna is the agent of destruction as well as of creation. This places the war between the Pandavas and the Kauravas in an altogether new light. The great battle to come should be seen as a moment in the cyclical world-process, an immense bloody sacrifice that will pave the way for a new creation. It also clarifies Arjuna's role as a combatant in that larger scheme of things. Krishna explains:

> Even without you all these warriors
> facing each other will cease to exist.
>
> And so stand up, Arjuna, seize the glory!
>   Conquer the enemy and enjoy kingship.
> These men have already been destroyed by Me.
>   Merely be My instrument, O great Archer. (11.32–33)

If the war is a sacrifice directed by the Supreme Being, then Arjuna should see himself as an "instrument" of the divine will carrying out the destructive rite. Arjuna's class duty as a Kshatriya warrior, engaging in a just war, is transfigured into an act of devotion within Krishna's cosmic plan.

Krishna's effort to persuade Arjuna to take part in the upcoming battle reaches its culmination in the Supreme Form he allows Arjuna to see. Arjuna may be persuaded now, but the dialogue does not end. Once Arjuna has regained his wits, he recommences his queries, and Krishna patiently answers. From this point, the dialogue has more the nature of a catechism, with Krishna recapitulating and amplifying his main points and extending them in new directions. Krishna provides another ranking of the methods of spiritual attainment, and he reformulates the nontheistic Samkhya ontology in theistic terms, with himself as the emanating center of all souls.

Krishna also takes up the subtle matter of the *gunas*, the basic qualities or characteristics of all matter. The Samkhya school postulated that all material nature is characterized by three *gunas: sattva* is described as pure and luminous, *rajas* is active and passionate, and *tamas* is lethargic and torpid. Insofar as we are embodied beings, each of us is made up of these three qualities in various mixtures. Some persons are more pure than others, some appear more passionate, and still others may tend to the laziness of *tamas*. It might appear that these qualities are ranked, with *sattva* the highest and *tamas* at the bottom. But all three *gunas*, Krishna explains, bring about bondage of the soul.

> *Sattva, rajas, tamas—gunas*
> material nature has produced—
> bind down *Atman* in the body,
> though it is imperishable. (14.5)

Therefore, the path to the highest attainment requires "going beyond these three *gunas*" so that the liberated soul may attain immortality (14.20). Arjuna again asks Krishna for a description of such a person, and Krishna portrays that one in much the same way he earlier described the *sthitaprajna*, in whom wisdom stands firm.

> Seated apart, dispassionate,
> undisturbed by the *gunas*,
> calmly watching *gunas* working,
> standing firm, never wavering,
>
> Self-contained, to whom pain and pleasure,
> a clod, a stone, a lump of gold,
> loved, and unloved are all equal, . . .
>
> he is said to transcend the *gunas*. (14.23–25)

Equanimity, dispassion, and service to Krishna through the *Yoga* of Devotion all lead to this place of perfection.

Krishna also takes up again the question of moral conduct. Earlier in the dialogue, Arjuna had asked what causes a person to commit evil (3.36). To address the problem, Krishna proposes a binary division of moral qualities into the "divine" and the "demonic" (16.1–4). Among the divine are virtues like self-control, liberality, nonviolence, truthfulness, and the like. The demonic, not surprisingly, are their opposites: deceit, pride, conceit, anger, ignorance. These sets of qualities lead the person in opposite directions, the divine toward freedom and the demonic toward greater bondage. Desire is at the root of the problem. So obscured is the knowledge of some demonic people, Krishna explains, that they identify desire not as an enemy, but as the foundation of the world. This is a grave error.

> Bound by a hundred snares of hope,
> devoted to desire and anger,
> they strive to gratify their desire
> with hoards of wealth unjustly gained.
>
> "This is what I obtained today;
> I will gratify this desire;
> This is now mine, and that also
> will be added to my riches;
>
> That enemy has been killed by me,
> and I will kill others as well;
> I am a lord, and I enjoy
> success, power, and happiness;
>
> I am wealthy and highborn.
> Who else is my equal? I will
> offer sacrifice, donate, rejoice."
> This is how they are deluded. (16.12–15)

Desire, anger, and greed are the three gates to hell. This might sound like a gloomy commentary concerning human nature, readily applicable to our own times. Krishna does intend it as a universal analysis, but it also returns Arjuna to the powerful forces that have brought him and his family to the hellish field of battle. The desire for kingship, the anger over personal slights and humiliations, and the greed for land and wealth have all taken their toll on the Kauravas and the Pandavas, leading them to Kuruskhetra.

At the end of the conversation, Krishna returns to the importance of duty and the renunciation of self-interest which turns action into "nonaction" without karmic bondage.

> With intellect always unattached,
> with self conquered, desire dispelled,
> one attains by renunciation
> perfect, unexcelled nonaction. (18.49)

But the performance of *dharma* without attachment, worthy as it is, is now subordinate to another virtue, that of *bhakti* or devotional adherence to Krishna as the Supreme.

> And, performing every action
> always with reliance on Me,
> from My grace one attains the eternal
> and imperishable abode.
>
> Concentrating on renouncing
> all action in Me as supreme,
> relying on *Buddhi Yoga,*
> constantly keep your thoughts on Me. (18.56–57)

This battlefield dialogue begins with Arjuna's grief and his confusion about his duty. To persuade Arjuna to engage in the looming battle, Krishna mobilizes a great variety of arguments concerning the soul, the ethics of action, the problem of bondage, and the paths of spiritual attainment. He reveals himself to be a new Supreme Being, both in words and in vision, and he instructs Arjuna in the liberating power of devotion to this God, a new and most effective route to the highest goal. "Have your ignorance and delusion been destroyed?" (18.72) Krishna asks at the end of his teachings. And the Kshatriya warrior replies:

> My delusion is gone; I have gained
> wisdom through Your grace, O Krishna,
> and am standing with doubt dispelled.
> I will carry out Your orders. (18.73)

The Great Battle and Its Aftermath

As soon as he completes his conversation with Krishna, Arjuna picks up his bow and arrows. Warriors cheer their approval. Drums of all sorts, cymbals, conches, and cow-horns raise a tremendous tumult. Even Indra and the other gods gather at Kurukshetra to watch the great battle about to commence. The interlude that was the *Bhagavad Gita*, a moral and theological dialogue examining the broader ramifications of the war, is over, and the battle may be joined in earnest.

This moment of celebration does not last long. Krishna may persuade Arjuna to fight and provide new ways for him to understand and justify his acts, but the fight to come and the *Mahabharata* narrative as a whole force Arjuna, the Pandavas, and the reader to recognize the terrible cost of these actions. The demonic qualities of insatiable desire, anger, and greed, which Krishna has identified as the threefold gateway to hell, take the field along with the warriors, and Arjuna's gruesome vision of world destruction is enacted on the battlefield.

As with many real-world wars, a military struggle that begins with hopes of glory and careful observation of the proper rules of engagement deteriorates into brutality and ends in catastrophic devastation. As the eighteen-day battle continues and casualties mount on both sides, the combatants resort to any means necessary to defeat their opponents. Many of the more egregious violations of the battlefield code of conduct are carried out by the Pandavas, with the encouragement of their advisor Krishna. They strike down their most formidable enemies when those fighters are immobilized or weaponless. They employ a blatant falsehood to demoralize their former teacher, Drona. Arjuna's brother Bhima drinks the blood of one Kaurava opponent, then murders Duryodhana with a mace-blow below the belt. On the eighteenth day the Kaurava warrior Ashvatthaman, Drona's grieving son, bitterly cites these Pandava transgressions to rationalize a devastating night raid of revenge on the Pandava camp, in which he and two cohorts assassinate thousands of enemy soldiers in their sleep, including all the sons of the five Pandava brothers and their wife Draupadi.

By the end of the Bharata war enormous numbers of warriors lie dead. Yudhishthira's post-battle tally holds that over one-and-a-half billion men have been killed, and twenty-four thousand gone missing. Their corpses cover Kurukshetra, along with the carcasses of elephants and horses. Hordes of jackals, ravens, crows, vultures, eagles, goblins, ghouls, and flesh-eating demons scavenge the fields. Almost all the males of the Kshatriya class of India have been wiped out. Their women are allowed onto the plain, wailing like ospreys, to look for the bodies of their fallen husbands, brothers, fathers, and sons. The corpses are then piled high atop a great pyre of broken weapons and wooden chariots for a gigantic mass cremation, and the women perform libations for the dead in the Ganges River. Gandhari, bereaved mother of one hundred Kaurava sons all now deceased, curses Krishna for his role in the battle. The resentments and recriminations over responsibility for this holocaust and the collective mood of profound grief are unbearable.

If the *Bhagavad Gita* begins with Arjuna's anticipatory grief and anxiety, it is not surprising that many of the concerns of that dialogue should continue to echo in the trauma-filled period of restoration after the war. Later echoes select and emphasize different aspects of the complex dialogue of the *Gita*. The *Gita* echoes at greatest length in Bhishma's discourse to Yudhishthira, the eldest of the Pandava brothers, to persuade him to take up his duties as ruler of the kingdom. It does so, in a more theistic vein, when Krishna, on his way home to Dvaraka, encounters the desert hermit Uttanka, who in his retreat has not heard about the war. When Uttanka threatens to curse Krishna for failing to stop the terrible slaughter, Krishna reveals himself as the Supreme Being and complies with Uttanka's request to see his Lordly Form, "the same one Arjuna has seen" (*MBh* 14.54.4). This is enough to demonstrate to Uttanka the futility of his curse, and as an already truly wise renouncer he does not require further instruction from Krishna in the importance of discipline or the path to salvation.

The message of the *Gita* is not even fully remembered by its original audience, Arjuna. The Pandava warrior lives a comfortable post-war life in the new imperial kingdom established by his older brother, but he continues to have bouts of grief and trauma. When Krishna visits, Arjuna confesses that he can no longer recall just what Krishna told him at Kurukshetra.

> Krishna, son of Devaki, when the battle was just about to begin, I perceived your greatness and your Lordly Form. But what you told me then out of friendship, Krishna, all that has disappeared from my damaged mind. And I am curious again about these matters, Krishna, and you will soon be leaving for Dvaraka. (*MBh* 14.16.5–7)

Krishna is disappointed and chastises his friend.

> You heard a secret from me and learned about the eternal, about *dharma* in its inherent form, and about all the eternal worlds. It is very

disagreeable to me that you have not grasped it due to your ignorance.
You are certainly faithless and dull-minded, Arjuna. (*MBh* 14.16.9–10)

He adds that it is not possible now for him to repeat exactly what he told
Arjuna at that time. Arjuna's situation is different now, and Krishna no
longer has the same compelling interest in Arjuna performing his duty as a
Kshatriya. Krishna does go on to deliver another lengthy discourse to Arjuna,
which came to be called the *Anugita*, the "after-Gita" or secondary Gita. In
this latter song, though, Krishna simply reports other dialogues between
other teachers and students, rather than speaking in his own voice. And this
discourse takes up only some of the themes of the more complex battlefield
dialogue, while deemphasizing or ignoring others.

Fortunately, later audiences have not had to rely on Arjuna's defective mem-
ory or Krishna's partial recapitulation of that earlier discourse. The courtier
Sanjaya has observed and heard the entire dialogue of Krishna and Arjuna at
Kurukshetra with the aid of divine eyesight granted to him by the sage Vyasa.
On the tenth day of the battle, this temporarily omniscient narrator returns
to Hastinapura to report to his master, the blind ruler Dhritarashtra, father
of Duryodhana and the other Kaurava brothers. Naturally Dhritarashtra has
a compelling interest in everything that has happened at Kurukshetra. The
Bhagavad Gita is framed as one small portion of Sanjaya's lengthy divine-
eyewitness report of the entire Bharata war.

In that account, as soon as Krishna concludes his final instructions, and
Arjuna pronounces himself fully convinced and ready to fight, Sanjaya speaks
up in his own voice.

> By Vyasa's grace I have heard
> this supreme and secret *Yoga*
> that Krishna, the Lord of *Yoga*
> Himself, divulged before my eyes.
>
> O King, each time I remember
> this miraculous dialogue
> between Arjuna and Krishna,
> I rejoice again and again. (18.75–76)

Sanjaya, then, is the first one to hear and rejoice over Krishna's teachings at
Kurukshetra, but by no means the last. The sage Vyasa—who is also biological

grandfather of both the Pandavas and Kauravas—subsequently compiles Sanjaya's narration of the battle with many other materials and assembles or composes the great epic of the Bharata clan, its fall and restoration. Vyasa teaches the composition to his five pupils, including a young Brahmin named Vaishampayana.

Many years after the epochal battle, Arjuna's great-grandson King Janamejaya decides to hold a giant snake sacrifice. To avenge the death of his father, who died from a snakebite, Janamejaya seeks to destroy all the snakes in the world through this yearlong ritual. Vyasa and his pupils attend the sacrifice, and in the long periods between rites, Vaishampayana recites to Janamejaya the epic story. Vyasa is present at this colloquy, but apparently he never needs to correct his diligent student. A wandering bard, Ugrashravas, also listens with great interest and superior retentiveness. Ugrashravas then makes a pilgrimage to Kurukshetra and later retells Vyasa's great composition, the *Mahabharata*, to a group of Brahmin anchorites undertaking a twelve-year sacrifice in the Naimisha Forest. This, in any case, is the account the *Mahabharata* tells of its own composition.

Composition and Transmission

Modern Indological scholars have developed a different hypothesis of how the *Mahabharata* and the *Bhagavad Gita* came into being. But much like the *Mahabharata's* own account of multiple oral recitations over several generations, most scholars assume that the massive epic as we have it was assembled and composed gradually though oral recitation before eventually being committed to written form.

Some Indological scholars speculate that the story may have originated with persons and events dating back to around 900 BCE. They cite genealogical, archeological, and linguistic evidence for this. Historically, this was a pre-urban period of largely nomadic Indo-Aryan tribes migrating into the Indo-Gangetic plains of northern India. Oral tales celebrating a great battle between contending chieftains among Indo-Aryan tribes may have circulated among bardic storytellers attached to the warrior clans. The consensus of scholars, however, holds that the Sanskrit *Mahabharata* available to us does not come from that time. The social organization in the epic, and the fundamental concerns and themes that the epic addresses, reflect a much later stage in Indian history.

The crucial period in which the *Mahabharata* was consolidated as a complex but unified epic poem, most scholars now agree, came during a period of religious and political contention. Starting around the sixth century BCE, ascetic movements growing out of the teachings of figures like the Buddha Shakyamuni and the Jina Mahavira offered a fundamental religious challenge to the claims and status of orthodox Vedic Brahmins. And within the Mauryan empire, which succeeded in uniting almost the entire Indian subcontinent within a single imperial polity, rulers adopted the guidance and many of the ideas of the heterodox leaders. The most famous among them, Ashoka Maurya (r. 269–232 BCE), converted to Buddhism after a victorious campaign and a particularly bloody war in Kalinga (modern Orissa), and he proclaimed his own principles of *dharma* in edicts promulgated throughout the Mauryan domain. One primary impetus for the composition of the *Mahabharata* was to counter the heterodox challenge, to reassert the privileged status of Brahmins, and to reflect on the ethics and pragmatics of Kshatriya power, all within a deeply compelling story of war. Scholars therefore locate the primary period of epic consolidation in the immediate aftermath of Mauryan rule, from around 200 BCE to the beginning of the Common Era. The *Mahabharata* offered itself as a "Fifth Veda," a new articulation of Truth for the new age, an inspired work that would serve, as James Fitzgerald puts it, "as a comprehensive Brāhman-inspired basis for living a good life in a good society in a good polity."[2]

This post-Mauryan composition was not the final draft, however. Whether oral or written, this first recension remained a somewhat open text. For several centuries, those who transmitted the epic felt free to incorporate revisions and additions that would enhance the central narrative and keep it up to date. We cannot fully reconstruct the editorial process by which new materials were evaluated and either allowed to remain or deleted. We do not have any rough draft to compare with the final version.

At some point, most likely between 300 and 450 CE, a single authoritative version of the *Mahabharata* was finalized, written down, and disseminated widely. It may well have been done under the aegis of the Gupta empire

---

2. Fitzgerald, James L., "Mahābhārata," in *The Hindu World*, ed. Sushil Mittal and Gene Thursby (New York: Routledge, 2004), 54.

(320–547 CE). Gupta rulers portrayed themselves as restorers of Vedic traditions and followers of the god Vishnu, and a powerful Fifth Veda fit well within their ruling agenda. This authoritative version evidently replaced any other existing recensions or consigned them to palm-leaf oblivion. (In the Indian climate, palm-leaf manuscripts deteriorate within a century or two, and texts must be recopied in order to survive.) When scholars at the Bhandarkar Oriental Research Institute in the early twentieth century collected hundreds of manuscript versions of the *Mahabharata* from all parts of India and beyond, they determined that all the manuscript lineages descended from a single source. The critical edition of the epic they derived and published in twenty hefty volumes between 1933 and 1966 is, we must assume, a close approximation of this Gupta-era final draft.

When we turn to the *Bhagavad Gita*, similar compositional questions linger. The name "Krishna" may turn up in a few early sources, but as the divine charioteer and teacher of Arjuna in the *Mahabharata*, Krishna is a literary character of a much later time. Some scholars have asserted that the *Bhagavad Gita* was originally an independent composition that was simply incorporated into the epic. It is better, I believe, to follow the lead of J. A. B. Van Buitenen, the Indologist who translated the first five books of the *Mahabharata* as well as the *Bhagavad Gita*.

> The *Bhagavadgītā* was conceived and created in the context of the *Mahābhārata*. It was not an independent text that somehow wandered into the epic. On the contrary, it was conceived and developed to bring to a climax and solution the dharmic dilemma of a war which was both just and pernicious. The dilemma was by no means new to the epic, nor is it ever satisfactorily resolved there, yet the *Gītā* provides a unique religious and philosophical context in which it can be faced, recognized, and dealt with.[3]

Composed within the *Mahabharata* as a profound reflection on the dilemma built into the central narrative, the *Bhagavad Gita* most likely dates to the first two centuries of the Common Era.

Krishna's teachings are clearly embedded in the larger narrative, and through them he achieves his immediate aim of persuading Arjuna to take

---

3. Van Buitenen, J. A. B., *The Bhagavadgītā in the Mahābhārata* (Chicago: University of Chicago Press, 1981), 5.

part in battle. But Krishna makes it clear that he also has broader aspirations in mind for this dialogue. However grounded it may be on the Kurukshetra field of battle, it also has a universal bearing. It is worthy of being remembered, recited, and heard by future audiences, as he stresses:

> Whoever sets forth this highest,
> secret teaching to My votaries,
> and has worshipped Me devoutly,
> will come to Me without a doubt. (18.68)

To transmit his teachings, Krishna promises, is an act of *bhakti* leading to union with God. It is also a form of *Jnana Yoga*.

> Whoever studies and recites
> this sacred dialogue of ours,
> will have cherished Me, I avow,
> with the sacrifice of wisdom. (18.70)

Krishna envisions that his battlefield conversation with Arjuna will enjoy a long life through the beneficial human activities of recitation and reception. And of course he has been proven correct.

The *Bhagavad Gita* may have been composed as an integral portion of the larger epic poem, but it also circulated as an independent work from an early period. Even if it did not wander into the *Mahabharata*, it did wander out. In medieval India, philosophers representing various schools of thought considered Krishna's teachings to be one of three textual foundations for setting forth their own philosophical positions, and they composed deeply learned commentaries on the work. Writing in the early ninth century, the great Advaita Vedanta (non-dualist) philosopher Shankara held that the *Bhagavad Gita* contained the concentrated essence of the Vedas. But he also observed that this essence was not so easy to discern.

> Now this treatise called the *Gita*, which contains the concentrated essence of the meaning of the Vedas, is difficult to understand. Even though many commentators have explained the meanings of each word, the meaning of its sentences, and its overall plan in an effort to reveal its true meaning, the general public still perceives the work as conveying multiple meanings, and very contradictory ones at that.

Recognizing this situation, I will compose a succinct exposition of the *Gita* in order to determine its true meaning through discrimination.[4]

Just as Shankara set out to supplant previous commentaries, other teachers would in turn compose new ones to clarify or to combat Shankara's exposition. So in the eleventh century Ramanuja wrote a new explanation from a Vishishtadvaita Vedanta (qualified non-dualist) perspective, and in the thirteenth century Madhva contested both of these predecessors from a Dvaita Vedanta (dualist) position—to name only the best-known commentaries. A recent compilation found 227 extant Sanskrit commentaries on the *Bhagavad Gita*. The true meaning of Krishna's teachings was evidently up for grabs, as exponents of widely divergent schools all found in the work validation for their own distinctive tenets.

In 1785 a British colonial officer serving in Calcutta, Charles Wilkins, working closely with the distinguished Brahmin pundit Kashinatha Bhattacharya, translated the *Bhagavad Gita* into English. Based on his conversations with his Brahmin teachers, Wilkins proclaimed the *Gita* to be the key to understanding Hinduism. "The Brahmans esteem this work to contain all the grand mysteries of their religion," he wrote in his preface.[5] Published in London, it was the first work of classical Sanskrit to appear in English. The translation quickly spread through learned circles in Europe and provoked fascination and admiration among the savants. Enthusiasm for this and other Sanskrit translations that soon followed led some to see ancient India as the very source of world civilization. The German poet and literary critic Friedrich von Schlegel exclaimed in a letter to a friend, "Here is the actual source of all languages, all the thoughts and poems of the human spirit; everything, yes, everything without exception has its origin in India."[6]

Wilkins's translation was the first, but by no means the last, to introduce Krishna and his teachings to an audience beyond India. The *Bhagavad Gita* has since appeared in translations in over seventy-five languages outside the subcontinent. In English alone, well over three hundred translations

---

4. Śaṅkara, *Bhagavadgītābhāṣya*, 1-2, in Richard H. Davis, *The Bhagavad Gita: A Biography* (Princeton: Princeton University Press, 2015), 54.

5. Wilkins, Charles, *The Bhagavat-gēētā, or Dialogues of Kreeshna and Arjoon* (London: C. Nourse, 1785), 23.

6. Schwab, Raymond, *The Oriental Renaissance: Europe's Rediscovery of India and the East, 1680–1880* (New York: Columbia University Press, 1984), 71.

have been published. It is by far the best-known Hindu work throughout the world.

Meanwhile in India, the popularity of the *Bhagavad Gita* has grown enormously over the past century and a half. In the early twentieth century, leaders of the struggle against British colonial power like Aurobindo Ghosh, B. G. Tilak, and Mohandas Gandhi took the *Gita* as a key Sanskrit work and utilized it to present their own programs for gaining independence and forming a new nation of Indian citizens. Myriad translations into every modern vernacular language of India and inexpensive editions by popular presses like the aptly named Gita Press have made the work easily available to a mass readership far greater than was ever the case before. Public recitations and expositions of the *Gita* by religious teachers are regular events in cities and towns throughout India. Modern interpreters adopt Krishna's principles in modern fields of endeavor, such as sports, business, and management. Indian political figures regularly praise the work, and some have proposed that the *Bhagavad Gita* be declared the "national scripture" of India (forgetting the fact that India is a constitutionally secular republic). It is clear that Krishna's hope that his sacred dialogue with Arjuna on the battlefield at Kurukshetra would be studied and recited by others in later times has come to fruition.

Stanley Lombardo's new translation of the *Bhagavad Gita* continues Krishna's hope for twenty-first-century English-speaking readers. He follows a long legacy of transmitters reaching back to legendary Sanjaya and Vyasa, and of English-language *Gita* translators starting with Charles Wilkins and Kashinatha Bhattacharya. Through translations, Krishna is still speaking. As a classicist and a noted translator of Greek epics, Lombardo combines a scholar's concern for accurate fidelity with a poet's sensitivity to sound and rhythm. We cannot really know what Krishna and Arjuna would sound like if they were to be reincarnated on some modern American Kurukshetra. But this translation perhaps can give us some idea.

Richard H. Davis
Bard College

TRANSLATOR'S PREFACE

The *Bhagavad Gita* is a poem embedded in a much larger poem, the *Mahabharata*, a war epic that is a distant Indo-European cousin to Homer's *Iliad*, a work central to my life as a poet-translator. When I began work on the *Gita*, I felt I was on familiar ground. The poem opens as the major battle of the *Mahabharata* is about to take place on Kurukshetra Field. It could as well be the plain of Troy, huge opposing armies drawn up for battle, with the heroes, each with their heroic epithets, lining up in their war chariots. And when Arjuna, the *Gita's* preeminent hero, refuses to fight, how can we not think of the great Achilles withdrawing from battle as the *Iliad* opens? But then of course each poem goes its own way. Achilles ignores all good counsel and fights again only to avenge the death of his beloved Patroclus. Arjuna, however, will return to do his duty in war after absorbing the lengthy moral teaching of his charioteer, Krishna, who gradually reveals himself to be the Supreme Being in all its awesome and terrifying splendor. A major part of the poetic genius of the *Gita* is that the urgent sense of high purpose, the epic strain that is given voice at the beginning of the poem, is sustained throughout the long and varied philosophical discourse that constitutes the poem's main body. Reproducing that voice in all its modulations has been my constant aim in this translation.

I have composed the translation in four-line stanzas that approximate the Sanskrit's quatrains' eight-syllable lines (*shloka*) and occasional eleven-syllable lines (*trishtubh*), keeping as close to the original text as I could given the differences in English and Sanskrit idiom and sentence structure. Along with accuracy, I have given close attention to readability, sensitivity to tonal range, and capturing some sense of the original's rhythmic movement. Above all I have tried to craft the verse to suit the needs of a performance text, whether as spoken word or in a musical setting.

My main departures from the text have been modification or omission of some of the numerous and often extravagant epithets of Krishna and Arjuna, which sometimes can create confusion and often serve as little more than metrical filler in the original text. As in my translations of Homeric epic, I have tried to preserve enough epithets to give the reader some sense of this stylistic feature while maintaining readability and clarity.

As an illustration of some of the issues involved—versification, sentence structure, and epithets and proper names—consider *shloka* 2.10. Below I have provided a transliteration of the Sanskrit text with an interlinear gloss, followed by my translation.

> *tam uvāca hirhsīkeshah*
> him spoke bristle-haired
>
> *prahasann   iva   bhārata*
> about to laugh as if Bharata
>
> *senayor   ubhayor madhye*
> of armies of both   in the middle
>
> *visīdantam idam vacah*
> despondent this   speech
>
> Then, O Bharata, Lord Krishna,
> a smile playing on his lips, spoke
> to the despondent Arjuna
> there between the opposing armies.

Versification: Sanskrit verse, like classical Greek and Latin verse, is based on syllable length rather than word accent as in standard English verse. A syllable is long if it contains a long vowel (marked by a macron in the sample above) or a vowel followed by two consonants. Although the syllable count is constant for each line, allowable metrical patterns vary considerably, though there is a tendency toward iambic rhythms. I have mingled trochaic and iambic tetrameter rhythms, staying close to natural English speech cadences, in my translation of the *shloka* quatrains, in which most of the *Bhagavad Gita* is composed (as well as almost all of the *Mahabharata* in which it is embedded). The eleven-syllable *trishtubh* lines, used in passages of heightened emotion and most notably in Arjuna's agitated reaction to Krishna's theophany in chapter 11, are translated into loose eleven-syllable lines with alternate lines indented to indicate the shift to this verse form.

Sentence structure: Sanskrit, again like Latin and Greek, is a highly inflected language, word endings rather than word order marking grammatical functions and relationships. This allows the poet to separate, for instance, an adjective from the noun or pronoun that it modifies. In this quatrain the accusative-case adjective *visīdantam* ("despondent") in the fourth line modifies the accusative-case pronoun *tam* ("him") in the first line, the delay of the adjective producing here a particular poignant effect that cannot be reproduced with natural English word order.

Epithets and proper names: Bharata (line 2) was an ancient king whose name is also applied to his descendants, including Arjuna and Dhritarashtra. Here it signifies the latter and is retained in the translation. "Bristle-haired" is an epithet of Krishna, whose proper name is used in the translation instead of the epithet for the sake of clarity.

Finally, the *Bhagavad Gita* contains a little over a hundred distinct proper nouns—names of heroes, deities, titles, places, and so forth. All these are identified and indexed in the Glossary. Also included in the Glossary are thirty-one technical terms (as distinct from proper names) that have been left in Sanskrit in the translation, where they are italicized: *ahamkara, asat, atman, bhakti, brahmin, buddhi, dharma, dhyana, guna, japa, jnana, kalpa, karma, kshatriya, nirvana, Om, prana, rajas, rishi, samsara, sat, sattva, shudra, soma, sutra, tamas, tat, vaishya, yoga, yogic, yuga.* These terms have precise and in some cases multiple meanings that do not map neatly onto the English lexicon. Words such as *yoga* (which occurs over sixty times) and *karma* have come into English but with a narrower and somewhat different range of meanings than in the *Bhagavad Gita.* Leaving these terms in Sanskrit with explanations in the Glossary results in a more economical translation and an opportunity for the reader to engage with the original language. It also presents readers with a challenge. When encountering even familiar-looking italicized words in the translation, readers are thus urged to consult the Glossary and not to rely on their knowledge of how the loanword is used in everyday English. Of the Sanskrit terms retained in the translation, the most frequently occurring—and the ones readers will likely profit most from familiarizing themselves with prior to reading the poem—are *dharma, guna, karma, rajas, sattva, tamas, yoga.*

I would like to thank first Richard Davis for his generous and illuminating Introduction and Afterword, as well as for the many helpful suggestions to improve the translation he made as a reader for the press. I am in debt also to another, anonymous, reader for the press for encouraging comments. My thanks also to Anna Mayersohn for her help in compiling the Glossary and Index and for proofreading the entire translation. I am grateful to Mary Kirkendoll for helping me examine key passages of the translation with a close eye on the Sanskrit text, and for hosting a public reading. Brian Rak, my editor at Hackett, having seen me through many an epic as well as a few lyric productions, has my deep gratitude once again. As does my wise and patient wife, Judy Roitman, as ever.

Note on the Text

This translation is based on the Sanskrit text of Winthrop Sargeant's edition (*The Bhagavad Gītā*, Albany: SUNY, 1994). I have made use of this edition's lexical and grammatical notes, and I have also consulted the commentaries by R. C. Zaehner (*The Bhagavad-Gita, with a Commentary Based on the Original Sources*, London: Oxford University Press, 1969) and Robert Minor (*Bhagavad Gita: An Exegetical Commentary*, New Delhi: Heritage, 1982).

—Stanley Lombardo

BHAGAVAD GITA

Chapter One

Dhritarashtra spoke:

"Tell me, Sanjaya, what my sons   *1*
and the sons of Pandu did
when they met arrayed for battle
on Kurukshetra's sacred plain."

Sanjaya answered:

"When King Duryodhana saw   *2*
the fighting force of Pandu's sons
he approached his teacher, Drona,
and addressed him with these words:

'Look, O master, at this army,   *3*
this great Pandava fighting force
marshaled by Drupada's son,
by your own sagacious student.

Here are heroes, mighty archers,   *4*
Arjuna's and Bhima's equals,
Yuyudhana and Virata,
and Drupada, great charioteer;

Dhrishtaketu, Chekitana,   *5*
the heroic king of Kashi,
Purujit and Kuntibhoja,
Shaibya too, a bull of a man;

mighty Yudhamanyu also,   *6*
and the powerful Uttamaujas,
Subhadra's son, Draupadi's sons,
all driving their great chariots.

And all of our most distinguished,　　　　　　*7*
know them, highest of the Twice-born!
All the commanders of my troops
I will now name for you to hear.

You, lord Drona, Bhishma, Karna,　　　　　　*8*
and Kripa the victorious,
Ashvatamma and Vikarna,
the son of Somadatta too,

and many other heroes who　　　　　　*9*
for my sake put their lives at risk,
both wielding and hurling weapons,
all of them veteran warriors.

Our forces under Bhishma　　　　　　*10*
do not measure up, are lacking.
But our forces under Bhima
do measure up, are sufficient.

In all movements and positions,　　　　　　*11*
in whatever places stationed,
all of you, protect old Bhishma,
do indeed protect him, lordships!'

Making Duryodhana happy,　　　　　　*12*
his grandfather, the aged Kuru,
made his conch horn roar like a lion,
full of dignity and power.

Then all the horns and kettledrums,　　　　　　*13*
the great cymbals and the trumpets
were struck and sounded all at once
with a din like rolling thunder.

And, standing in their chariot,　　　　　　*14*
mighty, yoked with silver horses,

Madhu's slayer and Pandu's son
sounded their own divine conch horns.

Krishna blew his horn Panchajanya,   *15*
Arjuna sounded Devadatta,
and terrible, wolf-bellied Bhima
blew his great conch horn Paundra.

Kunti's son, King Yudhishthira,   *16*
sounded Anantavijaya;
Nakula and Sahadeva blew
Sughosha and Manipushpaka.

The Kashi king, best of archers,   *17*
and the great warrior Shikandi,
Dhrishtadyumna and Virata,
and invincible Satyaki,

Drupada and Draupadi's sons,   *18*
all together, O Lord of Earth,
and Subhadra's strong-armed son—
each of them blew his own conch horn.

And the noise shattered the hearts   *19*
of the sons of Dhritarashtra,
the tumultuous sound echoing
throughout the heavens and the earth.

Then Arjuna, son of Pandu,   *20*
seeing the sons of Dhritarashtra
arrayed for battle, raised his bow
amid the first clash of weapons.

And he spoke these words to Krishna: *21*
'O Imperishable Lord of Earth,
draw my chariot to the middle,
station it between the armies.

Keep it there until I've surveyed   22
these battle-hungry warriors
with whom I must do combat soon
in this war we've undertaken.

I see men banded together   23
to do battle in the service
of Duryodhana, the evil-minded
son of King Dhritarashtra.'

And so Krishna, as requested   24
by Arjuna, O Dhritarashtra,
drew the chariot to the middle
of the two opposing armies.

Before the eyes of Bhishma, Drona,   25
and all these princes of the earth,
Arjuna, son of Pritha, spoke:
'Look at these assembled Kurus.'

Arjuna saw standing there   26
fathers first, and then grandfathers,
maternal uncles, teachers, brothers,
sons, grandsons, and friends as well,

Fathers-in-law and companions.   27
All of these in both the armies
the son of Kunti contemplated,
all his kinsmen arrayed for battle.

He was filled with boundless pity,   28
and in despair he spoke these words:
'Seeing my own people, Krishna,
drawing near in battle frenzy,

Both my legs collapse beneath me,   29
my mouth is dry, my tongue is cracked,

all my body shakes and trembles,
my hair bristles and stands on end.

My bow Gandiva falls from my hand,   *30*
and my skin feels like it's burning.
I cannot stand in position,
and my mind is wandering off.

I perceive bad omens, Krishna,   *31*
inauspicious, O Handsome One!
I foresee that no good can come
from killing my own kin in battle.

I do not desire victory,   *32*
hanker after royal pleasures.
What is kingship to us, Govinda?
What is luxury, or life itself?

Those for whose sake we desire   *33*
kingship, delicious food, pleasures,
stand here in battle formation,
forsaking their wealth and their lives.

They are teachers, fathers and sons,   *34*
grandfathers, maternal uncles,
fathers-in-law and grandsons too,
brothers-in-law and other kin.

I have no wish, Slayer of Madhu,   *35*
to kill those who are going to kill,
not even to rule the triple world,
much less to be an earthly ruler.

What joy would it give us, Krishna,   *36*
to kill Dhritarashtra's sons?
We would be beset with evil
if we killed our attackers here.

It is not just for us to kill   37
Dhritarashtra's sons, our kinsmen.
If we murder our own people,
could we ever be happy, Krishna?

There may be some people whose minds   38
are so overpowered with greed
they do not see that it is wrong
to betray and destroy their kin.

Do we not know enough, Krishna,   39
to turn aside from such evil?
To understand how wrong it is
to destroy friends and family?

With destruction of the family   40
ancient family customs vanish,
and lawlessness overpowers
the entire family structure.

When lawlessness reigns, O Krishna,   41
the family's women are corrupted,
and when they are corrupted, Krishna,
the castes become intermingled.

This intermingling hurls families   42
into hell with their destroyers,
and their ancestors are deprived
of their rice and water offerings.

Castes intermixed, families ruined—   43
when these crimes are committed
the duties of castes are abolished,
eternal family laws as well.

Men whose family laws are wiped out   44
dwell in hell indefinitely.

Have we not heard this repeated,
again and again, Lord Krishna?

Ah no! Alas! A great evil   45
is what we have resolved upon,
ready to kill our own people
out of greed for royal pleasures!

If the armed sons of Dhritarashtra   46
should kill me unarmed in battle
and offering no resistance,
for me that would be a happier fate.'

Saying this, Arjuna sat down   47
in his chariot on the field,
throwing down his bow and arrows,
his heart overcome with sorrow."

Chapter Two

Sanjaya went on:

Krishna, Slayer of Madhu, spoke   *1*
to the despairing Arjuna,
who was overwhelmed with pity
and whose eyes were brimming with tears:

"Why has this craven timidity   *2*
appeared at this critical hour?
It is ignoble, Arjuna,
and closes the gates of heaven.

Son of Pritha, do not give in.   *3*
This cowardice is beneath you!
Shake off this vile faint-heartedness
and rise up, O Scourge of the Foe!"

Arjuna answered:

"How can I fight back with arrows   *4*
against Bhishma in this battle?
Or Drona? Both of them deserve
my respect, O Demon Slayer.

Better to beg alms in this world than to kill   *5*
   my honored teachers. If I were to kill them,
however greedy for gain they now may be,
   all of my pleasures would be tainted with blood.

Nor do I know what would be preferable,   *6*
   to win or to lose. The sons of Dhritarashtra
stand here before us in battle formation.
   If I kill them, I will lose my will to live.

I am overwhelmed with a sense of pity,   *7*
     and my mind is confused as to my duty.
What would be best, I ask you? Tell me clearly.
     Advise me, your disciple, I beseech you.

I see nothing to dispel this grief of mine   *8*
     that drains my senses dry and saps their power,
not even if I were to obtain royal power
     unrivaled on earth, or lordship of the gods."

Sanjaya then said:

After Arjuna spoke these things   *9*
to Krishna, Lord of the Senses,
he added, "I will not fight,
Govinda," and then fell silent.

Then, O Bharata, Lord Krishna,   *10*
a smile playing on his lips, spoke
to the despondent Arjuna
there between the opposing armies.

And the Lord said:

"You mourn those who should not be mourned,   *11*
and yet speak as if you were wise.
But those who truly are wise mourn
neither the living nor the dead.

Never have I not existed,   *12*
nor have you ever not existed,
neither have any of these lords.
Nor will we ever cease to exist.

Just as our embodied being   *13*
goes through childhood, youth, and old age,
so too getting another body
is not confusing to the wise.

Sensory contact is the cause 14
of cold and heat, pleasure and pain.
Impermanent, they come and go.
You must just bear them, Bharata!

Bull of a Man, whoever remains 15
the same in happiness and grief,
disturbed by neither, such a sage
is fit for immortality.

In the unreal nothing exists, 16
and in the real nothing ceases.
Both these conclusions have been reached
by those who know the highest truth.

Know that what pervades the cosmos 17
is in fact indestructible.
No one is able to destroy
this imperishable being.

Only the bodies of the eternal, 18
indestructible, embodied Self
are said to die, come to an end.
Therefore, Arjuna, join battle!

Whoever thinks this embodied Self 19
is either the slayer or the slain
simply has not comprehended
that it neither slays nor is slain.

Neither is it born, nor does it ever die, 20
  does not come into or go out of existence.
Unborn, eternal, perpetual, primordial,
  it cannot be slain when the body is slain.

One who knows the indestructible, 21
the eternal, undying, unborn—

how can he cause one to be slain?
Whom, Son of Pritha, does he slay?

As, after casting aside worn-out garments,   22
    a person takes and puts on other, new clothes,
so too, after discarding worn-out bodies,
    the *Atman*, Self, encounters other new ones.

Weapons cannot cut or slash it,   23
nor can it be burned by fire;
water does not douse or drown it,
nor can it be withered by wind.

Not to be pierced, not to be burned,   24
neither to be drowned nor withered,
all-pervading and eternal,
it is unmoving and primeval.

It is said to be unmanifest,   25
inconceivable, unchanging.
If you understand it as such,
you are obliged not to lament.

And even if you think the Self   26
is constantly being born or dying,
even then, O Mighty Armed One,
you are obliged not to mourn it.

For all who are born, death is certain,   27
and birth is certain for the dead.
Since this cannot be avoided,
you are obliged not to mourn it.

Beginning as unmanifested,   28
beings then become manifest
and end as unmanifested.
What is there to lament in this?

There are some who perceive this as wondrous,   29
    there are others who say it is wondrous,
and still others who hear it as wondrous.
    But there is no one who understands it.

That which indwells every body   30
is inviolable forever.
You should therefore never lament
any being, O Bharata.

Perceiving your own proper duty,   31
you should not tremble or waver.
Nothing is nobler than rightful war
for those in the warrior class.

And if by good luck they attain   32
to the open gates of heaven,
warriors rejoice, Arjuna,
to have fought in such a battle.

If, however, you should refuse   33
to fight in this rightful battle,
shunning duty and glory both,
you will incur iniquity.

Everyone will talk about   34
your disgrace and shame forever;
ill repute is far worse than death
for whoever has known honor.

The great heroes will think that you   35
have held back through fear of battle,
and among those who esteemed you,
you will become of little worth.

And your enemies will say things   36
that should not be said about you,

mocking you and your prowess.
What suffering could be greater?

Slaughtered, you will attain heaven.   *37*
Victorious, you will enjoy earth.
Therefore rise up, son of Kunti,
Resolved now to enter battle!

Treating pleasure and pain the same,   *38*
gain and loss, victory and defeat,
join battle and engage in war!
Doing so you will incur no guilt.

Samkhya has made this clear to you.   *39*
Hear now insight into *Yoga*.
Practicing this, Son of Pritha,
will free you from all *karmic* bonds.

Effort is never wasted here,   *40*
nor is there any loss of ground.
Even a little of this practice
rescues you from great danger.

Arjuna, awareness must be   *41*
single-minded and resolute.
A mind whose attention wavers
divides and branches endlessly.

The ignorant all deliver   *42*
flowery speeches, Arjuna.
They delight in Vedic doctrine
and proclaim there is nothing else.

Greedily intent on heaven,   *43*
seeking rebirth as *karmic* fruit,
they perform abundant rituals
aimed at pleasure and at power.

Those attached to pleasure and power,   *44*
those perverted by this language,
do not achieve meditation
fixed in resolute awareness.

Indifferent to paired opposites
ignore the three Vedic *gunas*,   *45*
remain in goodness, free from greed,
and be completely Self-possessed.

As useless as is a wellspring   *46*
when the land is inundated,
equally useless are the *Vedas*
for a *brahmin* who knows the Self.

Your only right is to action,   *47*
never to the fruits of action.
Never give rise to this motive,
but don't be inactive either.

Do all things steadfast in *Yoga*,   *48*
without attachment, Arjuna,
the same in failure and success.
Yoga is equanimity.

Action is far inferior   *49*
to cultivation of the mind.
Take refuge in enlightenment.
Pity those seeking action's fruits.

The enlightened cast off in life   *50*
all acts of good and evil both.
Therefore yoke yourself to *Yoga*,
equanimity in action.

The truly wise, minds enlightened,   *51*
who have abandoned action's fruits,

But one who engages the mind   7
to curb the senses, Arjuna,
and to act in *Karma Yoga*
while unattached, is distinguished.

Do your duty, for action is   8
indeed better than nonaction!
Mere maintenance of your body
could not be done without acting.

Sacrificial action aside,   9
this world is constrained by action.
Act in order to sacrifice
without attachment, son of Kunti!

Prajapati, when he created   10
sacrifice along with humans,
said of old: 'Bring forth with this.
This will be your Cow of Plenty.'

May you sustain the gods with this,   11
and may the gods sustain you in turn.
By sustaining each other so
you will attain the highest bliss.

Sustained by sacrifice, the gods   12
will grant you all your desires.
If you enjoy these gifts without
giving in return, you are a thief.

The good, who eat the remains   13
of the sacrifice, are freed from ills.
The wicked prepare their own food
and eat their own foul suffering.

Beings exist because of food,   14
the origin of food is rain,

rain comes because of sacrifice,
the source of sacrifice is action.

Know that action comes from *Brahman*,   15
and *Brahman* from the Imperishable.
And so the omnipresent *Brahman*
becomes eternal in sacrifice.

Whoever fails to turn the wheel here   16
that has thus been set in motion
lives in vain, O Son of Pritha,
full of sensual pleasure and malice.

Whoever is pleased by *Atman*,   17
satisfied only by the Self,
content in *Atman*, such a person
has no need to engage in action,

Has no goal at all in action,   18
nor any goal in nonaction,
has no need of any being,
has no purpose whatsoever.

So being always unattached,   19
do, Arjuna, what must be done!
One who acts with nonattachment
surely will attain transcendence.

Janaka attained perfection,   20
and then others, by action only.
Just to hold the world together,
observe that you're obliged to act!

Whatever the greatest man does   21
all the others will imitate.
Wherever he sets the standard
the whole world will try to meet it.

As for Myself, there is nothing   *22*
in the three worlds for Me to do,
nothing at all to be attained,
and yet I act, O Arjuna.

If I were not at all engaged   *23*
in my weariless activity,
all the human race would follow
My example, Son of Pritha.

These many worlds soon would perish   *24*
if I were to keep from acting.
I would cause a cataclysm
and destruction of these creatures.

The unwise act from attachment   *25*
to their actions, O Bharata.
The wise should act without clinging,
intent on maintaining the world.

But do not shatter the unwise minds   *26*
of those still attached to action.
Cause them to enjoy all actions,
by your discipline and wisdom.

Every action is enacted   *27*
by the *gunas* born of matter.
Those deluded by the ego
think that they perform the actions.

But one who knows the dual roles   *28*
of the *gunas* and of action
stays unattached with just this thought:
'*Gunas* are at work with *gunas*.'

Those confused about the *gunas*   29
are attached to *gunas'* actions.
Those who know the whole should not
disturb dullards who know the part.

Entrust to Me every action,   30
meditate on the highest Spirit;
free from desire and selfishness,
fever broken, fight in battle!

Whichever human constantly   31
practices this teaching of Mine,
believing it, not disdainful,
is released from action's bondage.

But those who sneer at My teaching   32
and fail to put it into practice,
making a muddle of all wisdom—
regard them as lost and mindless.

Even the wise act in accordance   33
with their own material nature.
Beings follow material nature.
What then can restraint accomplish?

Passion and hatred are both seated   34
in the senses sensing objects.
Do not come under their power.
They are indeed your enemies.

Better your own duty poorly done   35
than doing another's duty well.
Better to die in your duty.
Another's duty is perilous."

Then Arjuna asked:

"What then can impel a person 36
to commit this harmful evil
even against his will, O Krishna,
as if he were compelled by force?"

And the Blessed Lord answered:

"Desire and anger are the force, 37
stemming from the *rajas guna*,
devouring and ruinous.
Know this as the great enemy.

As Agni is obscured by smoke, 38
or as a mirror is by dust,
an embryo by its membrane,
so the mind is dimmed by passion.

Even sages' knowledge is dimmed 39
by this eternal enemy,
manifested as desire,
a fire that is insatiable.

The senses, mind, and intellect 40
are said to be where it resides.
Along with these it confuses
the embodied soul, dims its knowledge.

Therefore, first control the senses, 41
O Bull of the Bharatas.
Kill this demon that destroys
knowledge and discrimination.

The senses are superior,
so they say, but mind is higher.
The intellect is higher still,
and the Self indeed much higher.

42

Having learned what is much higher,
sustaining the self by the Self,
kill the enemy that takes the form
of intractable desire!"

43

Chapter four

The Blessed Lord continued:

"First to Vivasvat, the Sun God,   1
I proclaimed this timeless *Yoga*.
Vivasvat to Manu taught it,
and Manu to King Ikshvaku.

The royal *rishis* understood   2
what they received in succession,
but after a long time on earth
Yoga was lost, O Arjuna.

It is just this ancient *Yoga*   3
that I am transmitting to you,
who are my friend and devotee.
This is the utmost secret teaching."

Then Arjuna said:

"But Your birth, O Lord, was later;   4
Vivasvat was born before You.
How am I to understand that
You taught this in the beginning?"

Krishna answered:

"Many of my births have passed now,   5
and many of yours, Arjuna.
I know all of my births, but you,
Great Warrior, do not know yours.

Though I am birthless and undying   6
and am the Lord of all beings,

by controlling My own nature
I come to be, through My own power.

Whenever *dharma*, or righteousness,　　　　　　7
decreases, O Bharata,
and unrighteousness increases,
that is when I create Myself.

For protection of the righteous　　　　　　8
and destruction of evildoers,
for establishment of *dharma*
I come to be from age to age.

And one who really knows the truth　　　　　　9
of My divine birth and action,
when he abandons his body
he is not reborn but comes to Me.

Gone is passion, fear, and anger　　　　　　10
for those who are absorbed in Me.
Many, purified through wisdom,
have attained My state of being.

Whoever comes to Me for refuge,　　　　　　11
in whatever way, I reward them.
Human beings everywhere
follow My path, Son of Pritha.

Desiring success through rituals　　　　　　12
men sacrifice to the gods here.
Ritual acts do bring success
quickly in the human world.

I created the four-caste system,　　　　　　13
balancing *gunas* and their actions.
And although I created this,
know Me as the Eternal Non-Doer.

I am untainted by action,   *14*
with no desire for action's fruit.
One who understands Me as such
is himself not bound by action.

The ancients, seekers of release,   *15*
knowing this engaged in action.
You too should engage in action
as in time past the ancients did.

What is action and nonaction?   *16*
Even the sages had this question.
After I explain this to you,
you will be released from evil.

First one must understand action,   *17*
and then understand wrong action,
and understand nonaction also.
Action's ways are deep and subtle.

One who sees nonaction in action   *18*
and sees action in nonaction,
such a one is accounted wise,
a *yogin* who performs all actions.

Those who have excluded purpose   *19*
and desire from their ventures,
their *karma* burnt in insight's fire—
the wise call such people sages.

Unattached to fruits of action,   *20*
always content, not dependent,
even while engaged in action
one does nothing whatsoever.

Mind indifferent, self restrained,   *21*
renouncing all acquisition,

acting only with the body,
one incurs no guilt in action.

Satisfied with whatever comes,   22
non-dual and free from envy,
constant in success and failure,
although one acts, one is not bound.

Attachment gone, liberated,   23
mind grounded deep in knowledge,
performing work as sacrifice,
one's *karma* wholly melts away.

Brahman is the offering, poured   24
by *Brahman* into *Brahman*'s fire.
Brahman will be attained by one
who sees in action only *Brahman*.

Some *yogins* offer sacrifice   25
to a god, while others offer
sacrifice through the very act
of sacrifice in *Brahman*'s fire.

Some offer senses such as hearing   26
in the fire of discipline;
others sensations such as sound
in the fire of the senses.

Others offer all sensory action   27
and the action too of *prana*
in *yogic* fire of self-restraint
that is kindled by deep knowledge.

Others offer their possessions   28
or their *Yogic* austerities;
ascetics offer Vedic study
and knowledge as their sacrifice.

Others offer exhalation,   *29*
inhalation, exhalation,
controlling the path of breathing,
intent upon *pranayama*.

Others, who restrain their diet,   *30*
offer prolonged inhalations.
All these understand sacrifice,
and sacrifice destroys their ills.

Enjoy the sacrificial nectar   *31*
and go to primordial *Brahman*.
Non-sacrificers lose this world.
How then do they gain the other?

There are many kinds of sacrifice   *32*
set before the face of *Brahman*.
Know that all are born of action
and you will be liberated.

Better than material sacrifice   *33*
is the sacrifice of knowledge.
Every action, Son of Pritha,
is fully understood in wisdom.

Understand that through prostrations,   *34*
humble inquiry, and service,
the wise will be moved to teach you
all that they know, O Arjuna.

With that knowledge you shall never   *35*
fall again into delusion,
and then you will see all beings
in yourself and in Me also.

Even if you were the most evil   *36*
of all evildoers and sinners,

you would, on the boat of wisdom,
cross beyond all iniquity.

As a kindled fire reduces   *37*
firewood to ashes, Arjuna,
so does the fire of knowledge
turn all actions into ashes.

Nothing in this world can be found   *38*
that purifies as knowledge does.
One who is perfected in *Yoga*
in time will find it in himself.

Those with faith will attain knowledge.   *39*
When that knowledge has been attained
and one holds fast, restrains the senses,
he soon will come to utmost peace.

Without knowledge and without faith   *40*
the one who doubts will be destroyed.
Neither this world, nor the one beyond,
nor happiness is for one who doubts.

Renouncing action in *Yoga,*   *41*
all his doubt cut off by knowledge,
such a person, Self-possessed,
is not caught in bonds of action.

Cut off with your sword of knowledge   *42*
the doubt that comes from ignorance
deep in your heart. O Bharata,
rise up now and practice *Yoga*!"

Chapter Five

Then Arjuna said:

"First you praise renunciation 1
and then you praise *Yoga*, Krishna.
Of these two, which is the better?
Give me a definite answer."

The Blessed Lord answered:

"Renunciation and *Karma Yoga* 2
both lead to highest happiness.
But of the two, *Karma Yoga*
is better than renouncing action.

The perpetual renunciant 3
neither hates nor desires,
is indifferent to opposites,
and with ease is liberated.

Samkhya and *Yoga* are different, 4
the childish say, but not the wise.
Either one correctly practiced
yields the fruit of both disciplines.

Those who follow *Samkhya* arrive 5
at the same place as *yogins* do.
Samkhya and *Yoga* are one thing.
He who sees this is one who sees.

Renunciation, Arjuna, 6
is difficult without *Yoga*.
The sage who is trained in *Yoga*
very quickly reaches Brahman.

One who is trained in *Yoga*,   *7*
whose self, subdued, cleansed, and conquered,
has become all beings' Self,
is not defiled even while acting.

"I do not do anything." Thus   *8*
thinks the *yogin* who knows the truth,
seeing, hearing, touching, smelling,
eating, walking, sleeping, breathing,

Talking, excreting, taking hold,   *9*
eyes opening and eyes shutting,
certain that the senses abide
in the objects of the senses.

Placing his actions onto Brahman,   *10*
having left behind all clinging,
his acts are unstained by evil
like a lotus unstained by water.

With body, mind, and intellect,   *11*
even with the senses only,
yogins act without attachment
so as to purify the self.

The trained *yogin*, abandoning   *12*
action's fruit, attains final peace.
The untrained, attached to the fruit,
is bound by action based on craving.

Renouncing all action in his mind,   *13*
the embodied soul sits happily
ruling the city of nine gates,
neither acting nor causing action.

The Foremost One does not create   *14*
the world's action or agency
or action's union with its fruit.
Nature itself keeps doing this.

Eternal Being does not receive 15
anyone's good or evil deeds.
Wisdom is veiled by ignorance,
and that deludes all who are born.

But for those whose ignorance of 16
Atman is destroyed by knowledge,
that very knowledge is like the sun,
illuminating the Supreme.

And those whose minds and selves are fixed 17
on That as the highest object
will never be reborn again,
their evils shaken off by knowledge.

The wise perceive the same *Atman* 18
in a cultivated *brahmin*,
in a cow or an elephant,
even in a dog or outcaste.

Even on earth rebirth is conquered 19
by those whose minds are set in sameness.
Brahman is impartial, spotless,
and therefore they abide in *Brahman*.

Not rejoicing at the desired 20
nor grieving at the undesired,
with mind firm and undeluded,
knowing *Brahman*, firm in *Brahman*.

Without clinging to sensations, 21
finding happiness in the Self,
through *Yoga* at one with *Brahman*,
one attains lasting happiness.

Pleasures born of sensory contact 22
are wombs of pain and suffering.
They start and stop, Son of Kunti.
The wise are not content with them.

One who is able to endure,   23
before release from the body,
distress born of greed and anger
is a disciplined, happy man.

A *yogin* with inner happiness   24
that comes from radiance within
is absorbed into *Brahman*
and attains *Brahman*'s *nirvana*.

Brahman's *nirvana* is attained   25
by seers whose evils are destroyed,
their doubts cut through, their selves restrained,
joyous in all beings' welfare.

For ascetics who have severed   26
desire and anger, thoughts controlled,
and who have knowledge of the Self
Brahman's *nirvana* is everywhere.

Banishing all outside contacts,   27
the gaze fixed between the two brows,
inhale and exhale equally,
breathing through the nostrils alone.

With senses and the mind controlled,   28
the sage who aims to be released
from desire, fear, and anger
is forever liberated.

By knowing Me, the Enjoyer   29
of sacrificial austerity,
the world's great Lord, the Companion
of all beings, he comes to peace."

Chapter Six

The Blessed One continued:

"He who performs the ritual   1
without attachment to its fruit
is a renunciant and *yogin*,
not he who neglects the ritual.

What is called renunciation,   2
that is *Yoga*, son of Pandu.
Without renouncing all desire
no one can become a *yogin*.

The sage who aspires to *Yoga*   3
attains it by activity.
One who has already attained it
maintains it by tranquility.

Clinging neither to sense objects   4
nor attached to any action,
renouncing purpose and desire,
one is said to have attained *Yoga*.

One should lift oneself by the Self   5
and not cause oneself to sink down.
The Self alone is oneself's friend
and oneself's only enemy.

The Self is a friend to whoever   6
has conquered himself with the Self.
For one who hasn't conquered oneself,
the Self remains an enemy.

One's self conquered, one's highest Self   7
remains at peace, immovable
in cold or heat, pleasure or pain,
whether honored or dishonored.

One content with knowing the Self,   8
unmoving, with senses conquered,
is called a *yogin*, one to whom
stones, clods, and gold are all the same.

Unbiased toward friends and enemies,   9
seeing kinsman and foe as equal,
impartial to the good and base—
such a person is preeminent.

A *yogin* should train constantly   10
to become at one with the Self,
in solitude, with mind controlled,
without desires or possessions.

Having set up in a clean place   11
a firm seat, neither high nor low,
a seat of kusha grass covered
with deerskin and soft cloth on top,

Sitting there and training his thought   12
on one point, controlling his mind
and his senses, let him practice
Yoga to purify his self.

With body, neck, and head erect,   13
remaining steady and unmoving,
gazing at the tip of his nose,
not looking around anywhere,

His self quieted, all fear gone,   14
firm in vows of celibacy,

with mind controlled, thoughts fixed on Me,
he sits steadfast, devoted to Me.

Practicing constantly in this way,   *15*
a *yogin* with his mind subdued
enters into supreme *nirvana*,
supreme peace, at one with Me.

Yoga means not eating too much,   *16*
but does not mean eating nothing,
not the habit of too much sleep,
nor, Arjuna, never sleeping.

For the one who is disciplined   *17*
in eating, in activity,
in sleep, and in being awake,
Yoga is destruction of sorrow.

When his mind is under control,   *18*
and he is absorbed in Self alone,
free of desire and of longing,
he is said to be a *yogin*.

As a lantern out of the wind   *19*
does not flicker, so too the mind
of the *yogin* does not waver,
steady in *Yoga* of the Self.

When his mind, restrained by *Yoga*,   *20*
becomes quiet in his practice,
when he himself perceives the Self
and in the Self becomes content,

He knows infinite happiness,   *21*
grasped by mind, transcending senses,
and, established in his practice,
does not deviate from thusness.

Having attained that, he cannot   22
imagine any greater gain.
Established there, he is not moved
even by profound suffering.

Let this unyoking from sorrow   23
be called *Yoga*, known as *Yoga*,
practiced with determination,
with a mind that is undismayed.

Having abandoned every desire   24
born of his will, each one of them,
the multitude of sense perceptions
restrained completely by his mind,

Little by little becoming still,   25
awareness firmly in his grasp,
his mind established in the Self,
he should not think of anything.

Whenever the unsteady mind   26
wanders away, moves to and fro,
he should restrain it, lead it back
to the Self to be controlled there.

His mind at peace, the *yogin* then   27
approaches happiness supreme,
all of his passions pacified,
free of evil, one with *Brahman*.

Practicing *Yoga* constantly,   28
the *yogin* then, free from evil,
readily encounters *Brahman*,
attaining boundless happiness.

The person trained in *Yoga* sees   29
the Self present in all beings

and sees all beings in the Self.
He sees the same Self everywhere.

He who sees Me in everything 30
and sees everything in Me,
that person is never lost to Me
and I am never lost to him.

The *yogin*, in oneness grounded, 31
who reveres Me as indwelling all,
whatever else he may be doing
continues to abide in Me.

The one who likens all beings 32
to his Self, sees them as equal,
whether in pleasure or in pain,
is thought of as a perfect *yogin*."

Arjuna then said:

"This *Yoga* of Equanimity 33
that you teach, O Slayer of Demons—
because of the mind's restlessness,
I do not see how to maintain it.

The mind, O Krishna, really is 34
restless, strong, and recalcitrant,
just as difficult to control,
I believe, as the wind itself."

Krishna answered:

"Without a doubt, mighty warrior, 35
the mind is restless, hard to restrain;
but through practice and dispassion
it can be brought under control.

I too think *Yoga* is difficult—   *36*
for one lacking self-control;
but through self-control and effort,
and skillful means, it can be attained."

Then Arjuna said:

"What about someone who has faith,   *37*
but his mind wanders, and he has not
reached the pinnacle of *Yoga*,
what end, O Krishna, does he meet?

Fallen from both paths, abandoned by   *38*
heaven and this world, O Krishna,
does he not vanish like a cloud,
deluded on the path to *Brahman*?

Dispel this doubt of mine completely,   *39*
as you ought to, O Lord Krishna,
for no one will come forth but you
who can cut through this doubt of mine."

And Krishna said:

"Neither in this world, Arjuna,   *40*
nor in the next does he perish.
No one who performs good acts
will ever come to grief, my son.

Having attained pure, righteous realms,   *41*
he will dwell there for countless years
after falling from *Yoga*'s heights,
then be reborn in a noble house.

Or he may even be reborn   *42*
in a family of wise *yogins*,

a birth that is very difficult
for one to meet with in this world.

He then connects with the knowledge   *43*
acquired in his former body
and strives harder than before
for perfection, O Arjuna.

He cannot help being borne along   *44*
by his practice in past lives.
Even the wish to know *Yoga*
is superior to the *Vedas*.

But it is the *yogin* who strives   *45*
for purity and perfection
assiduously through many births
who will reach the ultimate goal.

The *yogin* is superior   *46*
to ascetics, to the learned,
and to those who practice ritual.
Therefore, Arjuna, be a *yogin*.

And of all *yogins*, that one who   *47*
has great faith and whose inner self
is merged with Me, who worships Me,
is deemed by Me the most devout."

Chapter Seven

The Blessed Lord continued:

"With your mind absorbed in Me,   *1*
practicing *Yoga* intent on Me,
you will know Me, Son of Pritha,
wholly and beyond doubt. Listen!

I will completely explain to you   *2*
a discriminating knowledge
that, once it has been understood,
leaves nothing more to be learned here.

Of myriads of human beings   *3*
hardly any strive for perfection.
Of those who strive and are perfected
hardly any know Me as I am.

Earth and water, fire and wind,   *4*
space, mind, intellect, and ego:
My material nature is
divided into these eight parts.

That is My inferior nature,   *5*
but know that it is different from
My highest, spiritual nature
by which this universe is sustained.

My highest nature is the womb   *6*
of all beings. Understand this!
I am the origin and the end
of the entire universe.

There is nothing higher than Me,   *7*
O Arjuna, Wealth's Conqueror.
All that exists is strung on Me
like pearls and jewels on a thread.

I am the liquid taste of water,   *8*
the brightness of the sun and moon,
I am *Om* in all the *Vedas*,
sound in air, men's virility.

I am the earth's pleasing fragrance   *9*
the brilliance in the flaring sun.
I am the life in all beings
and the ardor in ascetics.

Know that I am the primal seed   *10*
of all beings, Son of Pritha,
the intellect of the intelligent,
the radiance of the radiant.

I am the might of the mighty,   *11*
free from passionate desire;
and I am the lawful desire
of those beings, O Bharata.

I am the *sattvic* qualities,   *12*
the *rajasic* and *tamasic*.
Know that these are from Me also,
not I in them, but they in Me.

The whole universe is deluded   *13*
by the threefold modes of being
caused by the *gunas*. It knows not Me,
higher than these and eternal.

This illusion, produced by Me   *14*
from the *gunas*, is indeed divine.

Only those who take refuge in Me
can pass beyond this illusion.

Wrongdoers, the lowest of men,   *15*
do not seek Me. They are deluded,
deprived of knowledge by illusion,
attached to a demonic life.

Among good men, there are four kinds   *16*
who honor me: those who suffer,
who seek knowledge, seek spiritual wealth,
and the wise man, O Arjuna.

Of these four, the man of wisdom,   *17*
steadfast forever, devoted to Me,
is foremost. I am dear to him,
and he is very dear to Me.

All of them indeed are noble,   *18*
but the wise man is thought to be
My very Self; his steadfast mind
abides in Me, the highest goal.

The wise man, after many births,   *19*
takes refuge in Me, thinking this:
'Vasudeva's son is all!'
Such a great soul is hard to find.

Men whose desires for this and that   *20*
have left them bereft of knowledge
resort to various gods and rites,
controlled by their material nature.

Whoever wishes to honor   *21*
whatever worshipped form with faith,
I bestow upon that person
a faith that is unshakable.

When one who is yoked to this faith 22
wants to beseech whatever form,
he receives from it his desires
because forms are ordained by Me.

But the fruit is impermanent 23
for those with scant understanding.
Those worshippers go to their gods;
My worshippers surely come to Me.

Though I am formless, the mindless think 24
that I have fallen into forms.
They do not know My higher being
is unsurpassed and eternal.

Veiled over in *Yogic* magic 25
I am not apparent to all.
This muddled world does not see Me,
birthless and imperishable.

I know those who have departed 26
and know the living, O Arjuna,
as well as beings yet to be,
but there is no one who knows Me.

Hatred and desire rising up 27
and the illusion of opposites
cause all beings, O Bharata,
to become deluded at their birth.

But those whose evil ways have ended, 28
those who are pure in their actions,
free from delusive duality,
worship Me with unyielding vows.

Those who depend on Me and strive   *29*
for release from old age and death
comprehend *Brahman* completely,
the highest Self, and all action.

They know I am the Supreme Being,   *30*
Supreme God, Lord of Sacrifice.
Even at the hour of death
their minds are steady, fixed on Me."

Chapter Eight

Arjuna then asked:

"What is *Brahman*, the Supreme Self? 1
What is action, O Highest Soul?
What is Supreme Being said to be?
What is the Supreme God said to be?

What is the Lord of Sacrifice 2
in this body, Slayer of Madhu?
And how, at the hour of death,
do the self-controlled come to know You?"

The Blessed Lord answered:

"*Brahman* is Eternal, Highest. 3
Supreme Self is the Inner Being
that produces creatures' beings.
Action is Creative Power.

Supreme Being is Existence. 4
Supreme God is Divine Agent.
The Lord of Sacrifice is Myself
here in this body, Arjuna.

He who dies remembering Me 5
as he abandons his body
proceeds to My state of being.
Of this there is no room for doubt.

Also, whatever state of being 6
he remembers as he expires,
he goes to that, Son of Kunti,
becoming just that state of being.

At all times, therefore, think of Me,   *7*
meditate on Me, fight to keep
your mind and intellect fixed on Me.
Then you will surely come to Me.

With mind tamed by *Yogic* practice,   *8*
with thoughts directed nowhere else,
one goes to the Supreme Spirit
in meditation, Arjuna.

By meditating on the primordial seer,   *9*
   the ruler that is subtler than an atom,
supporter of all, inconceivable form,
   the color of the sun, beyond all darkness,

At the hour of death, with mind unmoving,   *10*
   firm in devotion, and with *Yogic* power
channeling the breath between the two eyebrows,
   one will go to this divine Supreme Spirit.

What those who know the *Vedas* call the Eternal   *11*
   and which ascetics, free from passion, enter,
observing chastity to attain their goal—
   I will briefly explain that path to you soon.

Controlling all the senses' gates,   *12*
confining the mind in the heart,
placing vital breath in the head,
firm in *Yogic* concentration,

Chanting *Om*, the one-syllable   *13*
Brahman, meditating on Me,
such a one, renouncing the body,
goes forth to the ultimate goal.

The one whose thought never wanders   *14*
but has Me in mind constantly,

for such a devoted *yogin*
I am easy to reach, Arjuna.

Those great souls, drawing near to Me,   15
are not subject to rebirth,
that transient home of misery,
gone to the highest state of being.

Up to *Brahman*'s realm of being   16
the worlds return again and again.
But when I am reached, Son of Kunti,
there is no rebirth to be found.

Those who know that for Brahma   17
a day lasts one thousand *yugas*
and night lasts another thousand
understand what day and night are.

From the unseen all seen things come   18
at the arrival of Brahma's day.
At night's arrival they disappear
and again are known as the unseen.

The multitude of beings arise   19
and are dissolved over and over,
without their will, when night arrives,
and arise again at break of day.

But beyond this state of being   20
is another unmanifest state
higher than the primordial,
that does not perish when all else does.

This unmanifest state is called   21
the Eternal, the supreme goal.
Going there, they do not return.
That is My supreme abode.

This supreme Soul, Son of Pritha,   22
is reached by unswerving devotion.
All beings exist within it,
and it pervades the universe.

But of those times that the *yogins*   23
do return or do not return
when they depart, I will now speak,
O Bull of the Bharatas.

Fire, brightness, day, mid-month moon,   24
the six months of the northern sun:
those who depart during these times
and know *Brahman*, go to *Brahman*.

Smoke, night, the dark of the moon,   25
the six months of the southern sun:
attaining lunar light thereby,
the *yogin* returns, is reborn.

These two paths, light and dark, are thought   26
to be eternal for the universe.
Going by one he does not return,
by the other he returns again.

Knowing these two paths, Son of Pritha,   27
the *yogin* is not confused at all.
Therefore at all times you should be
steadfast in *Yoga*, Arjuna.

Having learned all this, the *yogin* goes beyond   28
    the pure, sacred fruit of Vedic study,
sacrifices, offerings, and austerities,
    and reaches the supreme, primordial state."

Chapter Nine

The Blessed One continued:

"But I will tell you, a believer,   *1*
a most secret combination
of knowledge and discrimination
that will release you from all evil.

This royal knowledge, royal secret,   *2*
is the supreme purifier,
righteous and intelligible,
both practical and eternal.

Those who have no faith, Arjuna,   *3*
in this teaching do not attain Me
and are reborn in the cycle
of *samsara*, death and rebirth.

The whole is pervaded by Me   *4*
in My unmanifest aspect.
Every being resides in Me;
I do not reside in beings.

Still, beings do not reside in Me.   *5*
Behold my great and lordly *Yoga*!
My Self causes and sustains beings
but does not reside in beings.

As the great wind goes everywhere   *6*
dwelling in space eternally,
in just this way all beings dwell
and exist in Me. Reflect on this.

All beings, O Son of Kunti,   *7*
enter my material nature
when a *kalpa* ends. I send them forth
at the beginning of a *kalpa*.

From My own material nature   *8*
I send forth again and again
this powerless multitude of beings,
empowered by My material nature.

And none of these actions bind Me,   *9*
O victorious Arjuna.
I sit aside indifferently
unattached to all these actions.

I oversee nature's creation   *10*
of the living and the inert.
This is the cause, Son of Kunti,
of the turning world's existence.

Deluded fools look down on Me   *11*
when I assume a human form,
ignorant of My higher being,
the great Lord of all beings.

Those of vain hopes and vain actions,   *12*
of vain knowledge, undiscerning,
live an evil, demonic life
and abide in deep delusion.

But those with great souls, Arjuna,   *13*
and of a celestial nature,
worship Me, have their minds on Me
as all beings' eternal origin,

Praising Me perpetually,   *14*
forging ahead with firm resolve,

honoring Me with devotion,
ever steadfast in their worship.

Others by knowledge-sacrifice   *15*
worship and acknowledge Me
as both the One and the Many,
multi-faced in all directions.

I am the rite and sacrifice,   *16*
the offering, the healing herb;
I am the sacred text, the ghee,
the fire and the poured oblation.

I am the universe's father,   *17*
mother, founder, and grandfather;
the known, the purifier, *Om*,
the *Rig, Sama, Yajur Vedas*;

The goal, supporter, lord, witness,   *18*
the home, the refuge, and the friend,
the origin, death, and foundation,
treasure house and eternal seed.

I am heat and I am the one   *19*
who withholds and sends forth the rain.
I am death and deathlessness both,
being and non-being, Arjuna.

Knowing the three *Vedas, soma* drinkers, cleansed,   *20*
   worship Me with sacrifices, seeking heaven.
Attaining the pure world of Lord Indra,
   they enjoy the gods' celestial pleasures.

Having enjoyed the spacious world of heaven,   *21*
   merit exhausted, they enter the mortal world.
Desiring pleasure, they come and they go,
   conforming to the law of the three *Vedas.*

For men who direct their minds to Me,   22
who worship Me with no other thoughts,
constantly united with *Yoga*,
I provide and preserve all they need.

Even those who worship other gods   23
and offer sacrifice in faith,
they also worship Me, Arjuna,
though not in an orthodox way.

I am indeed the Enjoyer   24
and the Lord of all sacrifice.
But they do not know Me truly,
and so they fall and disappear.

Adore the gods, go to the gods;   25
adore ancestors, to them go;
adore spirits, go to the spirits;
adore Me, surely come to Me.

A leaf, a flower, fruit, water   26
offered to Me with devotion
by anyone whose heart is pure
is an offering I accept.

Whatever you do, whatever you eat,   27
whatever sacrifice you make,
all of that, O Son of Kunti,
do as an offering to Me.

Free at last from the bonds of action   28
that produce good and evil fruits,
trained in *yogic* renunciation,
your freed self will surely find Me.

I am the same in all beings;   29
none are hated or prized by Me.

But those who are devoted to Me
are within Me, and I in them.

Even evildoers, if they   *30*
worship Me undividedly,
must be thought of as worthy souls,
having come indeed to right resolve.

Their souls soon become virtuous   *31*
and attain peace everlasting.
Be aware of this, O Arjuna!
No devotee of Mine is lost.

All those who take refuge in Me,   *32*
even if born from evil wombs—
women, merchants, even outcastes—
also attain the highest goal.

How much more so the pure *brahmins*   *33*
and the devoted royal seers!
Once in this transient, sorrowful world,
devote yourself to My worship.

Mind on Me, devoted to Me,   *34*
worshipping Me reverently,
holding Me as your highest goal,
your very soul will come to Me."

Chapter Ten

The Blessed Lord continued:

"Once again, Mighty Warrior,   *1*
hear from Me a sublime teaching
that I will give you, beloved one,
out of concern for your welfare.

Neither the multitudes of gods   *2*
nor the great seers know My origin.
I am the universal source
of all the great seers and the gods.

He who knows Me, the beginningless,   *3*
birthless Sovereign of the universe,
is undeluded among mortals
and released from every evil.

Acumen, knowledge, clarity,   *4*
patience, truth, self-control, calmness,
pleasure, pain, becoming, passing,
terror, and also fearlessness,

Nonviolence, fairness, contentment,   *5*
ardor, charity, fame, and shame—
all the various states of beings
come to exist from Me alone.

The seven great seers of antiquity   *6*
and the four ancestral Manus
from whom the world's creatures were born
came forth from Me, born of My mind.

Anyone who truly understands 7
My manifested *Yogic* power,
is without doubt united with Me
in unwavering, steady *Yoga*.

I am the origin of all, 8
everything comes forth from Me.
Knowing this the awakened ones
worship Me in meditation.

Concentrating their breath on Me, 9
awakening one another,
speaking about Me constantly,
they are content and full of joy.

Those who are steadfast in practice 10
and worship Me with affection,
I give to them *Buddhi Yoga*,
by means of which they come to Me.

Out of compassion for them I, 11
who dwell within their souls, destroy
the darkness born of ignorance
with the shining lamp of knowledge."

Then Arjuna said:

"Supreme *Brahman*, highest abode, 12
Purifier supreme, O Thou,
Spirit eternal and divine,
Primal God, unborn, pervasive:

Thus they call You, all the seers, 13
the divine seer Narada too,
Asita, Devala, and Vyasa,
and You Yourself tell me also.

I believe that all You tell me 14
is the truth, O Handsome-haired One.
None of the gods or demons know
Your manifestation, Blessed One.

You know Your Self through Your Self alone, 15
O Spirit Supreme, Lord of beings,
source of welfare for all beings,
God of Gods, O Lord of the world.

Please describe, for You are able, 16
the divine self-manifestations
by which You permeate the worlds
and maintain Your presence in them.

How may I know You, O *Yogin*, 17
through my constant meditation?
In what various modes of being
should I think of You, Blessed One?

Explain further Your *Yogic* power 18
and its manifestation, Krishna.
For I can never get enough
of hearing your immortal words."

And the Blessed One said:

"Listen! I will explain to you 19
My divine self-manifestations,
but only the main ones, Arjuna.
There is no end to My extent.

I am the Self, O Thick-haired One, 20
indwelling the hearts of all beings.
I am their beginning, and I am
their middle and their end as well.

Of the Adityas I am Vishnu.   *21*
Of lights I am the shining sun.
I am Marichi of the Maruts.
In the zodiac I am the moon.

Of the *Vedas* I am the Sama,   *22*
of the gods I am Vasava,
of the senses I am the mind,
beings' thoughts, and consciousness.

Of the Rudras I am Shankara,   *23*
the Yakshas' and Rakshas' Vittesha,
I am Agni of the Vasus,
of the mountains I am Meru.

Of household priests, know that I am   *24*
Brihaspati, O Arjuna.
Of commanders I am Skanda.
Of waters I am the ocean.

Of the great seers I am Bhrigu.   *25*
Of words I am the syllable *Om*.
Of rituals I am *japa*.
Of the unmoving, the Himalayas.

Of trees I am the sacred fig;   *26*
of divine seers I am Narada;
of the Gandharvas, Chitraratha;
of the perfected, wise Kapila.

Know that among horses I am   *27*
Ucchaishravas, born of nectar;
Airavata among elephants;
and among men I am the king.

Of weapons I am the thunderbolt;   *28*
I am Kamadhuk among cows;

I am Kama, the god of love;
of serpents I am Vasuki.

I am Ananta of the Nagas,   29
Varuna of aquatic creatures.
Of ancestors I am Aryaman;
of subduers I am Yama.

Of demons I am Prahlada;   30
of the reckoners I am Time.
Of animals I am the lion;
and of birds I am Garuda.

Of purifiers I am the wind;   31
of warriors I am Rama,
Makara among sea monsters,
and of rivers I am the Ganges.

I am the beginning and the end   32
and the middle of all creations.
Of knowing I am supreme Self-knowing,
I am the speech of those who speak.

Of letters I am the letter A,   33
the compound of compounded words.
I alone am infinite Time,
and I face in all directions.

I am death and the origin   34
of future things. Of feminines
I am fame, speech, prosperity,
memory, wisdom, courage, patience.

Of chants I am the Brihatsaman,   35
of meters I am the Gayatri.
Of months I am the Marga-shirsha,
of seasons the flowering spring.

I am the gambling of the cheats   *36*
and the brilliance of the brilliant.
I am victory and exertion,
the goodness of those who are good.

Of the Vrishnis I am Vasudeva,   *37*
of Pandu's sons I am Arjuna.
Of the sages I am Vyasa,
of poets I am Ushana.

Of kings I am their ruling power,   *38*
of the ambitious I am their counsel.
I am the silence of secrets
and the knowledge of those who know.

I am also what is the seed   *39*
of every being, Arjuna.
There is nothing, living or not,
that could exist except through Me.

There is no end to My divine   *40*
manifestations, Arjuna.
What I have listed are examples
of My manifestations' extent.

Every manifested being   *41*
that is powerful or glorious,
understand that all originate
from a fraction of My splendor.

But what good will all this knowledge   *42*
do you, Arjuna? I support
the entire universe constantly
with a single fraction of Myself."

Chapter Eleven

Arjuna then said:

"In kindness to me You have spoken   *1*
of the transcendent mystery
called the highest Self, the *Atman*.
This has cleared up my delusion.

Of beings' origin and passing   2
I have heard in great detail
from You, O Krishna, and have heard
of Your eternal majesty.

Just as You have described Your Self,   *3*
I would like, O highest Lord,
to look upon Your godly form,
O Spirit unsurpassable.

If You think it is possible   4
for me to see You like this, Lord,
then make Your everlasting Self
visible to me, God of *Yoga*."

The Blessed Lord said:

"Now look upon, son of Pritha,   *5*
My hundred, no, My thousand forms,
all My various shapes and colors,
all My divine appearances.

Look upon Indra's gods of storm,   6
roaring deities, gods of Agni,
celestial horsemen, many wonders
unseen before, O Arjuna!

Behold the entire universe   7
moving and unmoving at once
here in My body, Arjuna,
whatever you desire to see.

But you aren't able to see Me   8
with these natural eyes of yours.
I now give you an eye divine.
Behold My majestic power!"

Then Sanjaya said:

Having spoken in this way, O King,   9
Krishna, the great lord of *Yoga*
revealed to the Son of Pritha
his supreme majestic form,

A form of many mouths and eyes,   10
aspects many and marvelous,
multiple divine ornaments,
many divine brandished weapons,

Wearing godly clothes and garlands,   11
heavenly perfumes and ointments,
composed of marvels, a divinity
infinite in all directions.

If a thousand suns were to rise   12
all at once into the heavens,
such a brightness would resemble
the brilliant light of that Great Being.

What Arjuna was seeing there   13
was the entire universe
divided into many parts
in the body of the God of Gods.

Then Arjuna, who was so amazed   *14*
that his hair was standing on end,
bowed his head to the Deity,
and with palms joined said to Him:

"I see the gods in Your body, O Divine One,   *15*
    the gods and all kinds of beings assembled,
Lord Brahma seated on his lotus throne,
    all the seers, all the serpent divinities.

I see Your many arms, many bellies, faces, eyes,   *16*
    in every direction, an infinite form;
I see no end, no middle, no beginning,
    O Lord of All, whose form is all that is!

Crowned, holding a mace, bearing a discus,   *17*
    a mass of brilliance, radiant on all sides,
I see You, impossible to see completely,
    a luminous burning beyond all measure.

You are the fixed, supreme object of knowledge,   *18*
    You are the ultimate resting place of all,
You are the eternal protector of *dharma*,
    the primordial Spirit, I now understand.

Infinite power without beginning or end,   *19*
    with countless arms, the moon and sun Your eyes,
I see You, sacrificial fire in Your mouth,
    burning this universe with Your own splendor.

This entire space between heaven and earth   *20*
    is filled with You alone in all directions.
Seeing Your wondrous and terrifying form,
    the three worlds tremble, O magnificent Self!

Over there throngs of deities enter You.   *21*
    Some, terrified, bow reverently, praise You,

saying "Hail,"—throngs of great, perfected *rishis*
    singing Your glory with abundant praise.

The Rudras, Adityas, Vasus, the Sadhyas,   *22*
    the Vishves, the two Ashvins, Maruts, Ushmapas,
Gandharvas, Yakshas, Asuras, the perfected,
    all behold You with astonished wonder.

Seeing Your great form, Your many mouths and eyes,   *23*
    O Mighty One with many arms, legs, and feet,
many bellies, and mouths with terrible tusks,
    the worlds tremble at You, and I tremble too.

Reaching the sky, blazing with many colors,   *24*
    Your mouth gaping wide, Your huge fiery eyes—
having seen all this, my heart trembles and pounds.
    I've lost my nerve, I can find no peace, Vishnu!

Having seen all Your mouths with their many tusks,   *25*
    blazing like the fires that destroy time and space,
I don't know which way is which, I find no comfort.
    Have mercy, Lord of Gods, Abode of the World!

And going into You, Dhritarashtra's sons   *26*
    crowded in with all the rulers of the earth,
Bhishma, Drona, Karna, the charioteer's son,
    along with all of our foremost warriors.

They disappear quickly into Your mouths,   *27*
    Your terrible mouths, wide open and tusked.
Some of them are stuck between Your jagged teeth.
    I can see them there with their heads crushed in.

As all of the many rivers of the world   *28*
    rush down in torrents into the ocean,
so too all those heroes of the world of men
    hurry into the furnaces of Your mouths.

As moths or other insects fly directly 29
    into a flame and are swiftly destroyed,
so too entire worlds fly into Your mouths
    and to their instantaneous destruction.

Licking them up into Your fiery mouths 30
    You devour worlds from every direction.
Your terrible radiance fills the universe,
    burns and consumes it entire, O Vishnu!

Who are you, Lord of awesome form? 31
Homage to You! Be merciful!
I want to know You, Primal One;
I do not understand Your actions."

And the Holy One said:

"I am Time, mighty world-destroyer, 32
come to annihilate every world.
Even without you all these warriors
facing each other will cease to exist.

And so stand up, Arjuna, seize the glory! 33
    Conquer the enemy and enjoy kingship.
These men have already been destroyed by Me.
    Merely be My instrument, O great Archer.

Drona, Bhishma, Jayadratha, and Karna, 34
    and all the other heroic warriors
have been killed by Me. So do not falter. Kill!
    Fight! You will be victorious in battle!"

Then Sanjaya said:

After hearing this from the Handsome-haired One, 35
    Arjuna, who was now trembling in terror,

joined his palms, and bowing low to the ground
    stammered out in fright these words to Krishna:

"Rightly, Krishna, the universe rejoices   *36*
    and is delighted in rendering You praise.
Terrified demons flee in all directions;
    perfected beings in throngs bow down to You.

And why should they not bow to You, Great Being,   *37*
    greater even than Brahma the Creator?
Infinite Lord, You are the universe's home,
    eternal being and nonbeing and beyond both.

You are God primordial, ancient Spirit.   *38*
    You are the universe's supreme abode.
You are the knower, the known, the state beyond,
    pervading the universe, the infinite form.

You are Wind, Death, Fire, Water, and Moon,   *39*
    Lord of all creatures, the first great-grandfather.
All reverence to You a thousand times over,
    again and again all reverence to You!

Reverence to You from in front and behind,   *40*
    Reverence to You from all sides also, O All!
You are infinite valor, immeasurable might.
    Permeating all, You therefore are All.

For anything I've said thinking You just a friend,   *41*
    'Ho, Krishna,' 'Descendant of Yadu,' 'Comrade,'
anything not knowing Your majestic power,
    through negligence or even affection,

Making a joke, or disrespectfully,   *42*
    playing around, in bed, seated, or eating,
alone or even before others, Krishna,
    I ask for Your forgiveness, O Boundless One.

Father of the moving and the unmoving,   *43*
   venerated guru of the universe,
there is nothing like You in the three worlds,
   nothing greater, Incomparable Being.

Bowing down, therefore, prostrating my body,   *44*
   I beg forgiveness of You, Lord to be praised.
As a father to a son, as friend to friend,
   lover to beloved, please have mercy, God.

Seeing what has never been seen before   *45*
   I am excited, but my mind trembles in fear.
Show me, O God, the form You were in before.
   Be merciful, Lord, the universe's abode!

I want to see You as you were before, crowned   *46*
   with a diadem, armed with club and discus,
a figure with four limbs. Become that again,
   O Thousand-armed One possessing every form!"

The Blessed One spoke:

"This supreme form has been shown to you, Arjuna,   *47*
   by My grace and through My *Yogic* power,
a form of pure, infinite, primal splendor,
   never before seen by anyone but you.

Not by Vedic sacrifice or recitation,   *48*
   not by rituals, gifts, or austerities,
can I be seen like this in the world of men
   by any other man than you, Arjuna.

Do not tremble or be confused   *49*
seeing this sublime form of Mine.
Be free from fear, of cheerful mind.
See the form I am in again."

Having spoken in this way to Arjuna,   50
   Krishna showed him his familiar form again,
and the Great Soul's gentle, wondrous appearance
   brought peace and calm to his frightened spirit.

And Arjuna said:

"Seeing You in this pleasant   51
human form, O Lord Krishna,
my mind is now composed again
and my thoughts are back to normal."

The Blessed Lord said:

"This form of Mine that you've beheld   52
is difficult for one to see.
Even the gods long constantly
to catch sight of this form of Mine.

Not through study of the *Vedas*,   53
not through austere practices,
not by gifts or sacrifices
can I be seen as you have seen Me.

Only by unwavering devotion   54
can I be seen, O Arjuna,
can I be known, can be attained
in this way, O great warrior.

Doing My work, trusting in Me,   55
devoted to Me, without desire,
free from enmity toward all beings—
one comes to Me, Son of Pandu."

Chapter Twelve

Arjuna then asked:

"So, some committed devotees   *1*
worship You continually,
some the Eternal Absolute.
Which of these knows *Yoga* better?"

The Blessed Lord answered:

"Those who fasten their minds on Me   *2*
who worship Me continually,
endowed with supreme conviction,
are for Me the most devoted.

But those who worship the Eternal,   *3*
the Undefined, Unmanifest,
Omnipresent, Unthinkable,
the Constant and Immovable,

In control of all their senses,   *4*
even-minded on every side,
rejoicing in all creatures' welfare,
they indeed attain Me also.

Those focused on the Unmanifest   *5*
do meet with greater hindrances.
It is hard for embodied beings
to attain the Unmanifest.

But those who renounce all actions   *6*
in Me, holding Me as supreme,
who worship Me, meditating
on Me in unswerving *Yoga*,

I will soon deliver them, those   *7*
whose consciousness has entered Me,
from the ocean of death and rebirth,
O Arjuna, Son of Pritha.

So keep your mind on Me alone,   *8*
let your consciousness enter Me,
and then there is no doubt that you
will hereafter abide in Me.

If you prove to be unable   *9*
to keep your mind steady on Me,
then you can seek to attain Me
through constant practice of *Yoga*.

If you are unable to practice,   *10*
be intent on what My work is.
Even by performing actions
for My sake, you will be perfect.

If you cannot do even this,   *11*
rely on My *yogic* power.
Abandon all fruits of action
and then act, but with self-restraint.

Knowledge is better than practice,   *12*
meditation better than knowledge,
renunciation better still.
Peace follows renunciation.

A person who hates no being,   *13*
kindly and compassionate,
free from "mine" and without ego,
the same in pain and pleasure, patient,

A *yogin* always satisfied,   *14*
of firm resolve, with self-control,

whose mind is always fixed on Me
in devotion, is dear to Me.

One who does not shrink from the world,   *15*
nor the world from him, freed from joy,
from impatience, distress, and fear—
such a one too is dear to Me.

Whoever is impartial, pure,   *16*
able, free from anxiety,
without ambition, and is also
devoted to Me, is dear to Me.

One without either joy or hate,   *17*
without sorrow or desire,
beyond pleasant and unpleasant,
and devoted, is dear to Me.

The same toward friend and enemy,   *18*
the same in honor and disgrace,
in cold and heat, pain and pleasure,
liberated from attachments,

Silent in both praise and censure,   *19*
content with anything at all,
homeless, steady, and devoted—
such a person is dear to Me.

Those who honor the duteous way   *20*
to immortality just declared,
and who believe with devotion
I am Supreme, are most dear to Me.

Chapter Thirteen

Then Arjuna said:

"Matter and spirit, O Krishna,   *
the field and the field's knower,
knowledge and the act of knowing—
all this I wish to understand."

And the Blessed Lord said:

"This very body, Arjuna,   1
is declared to be the field.
Whoever knows the body is called
by the sages the field's knower.

Understand that I am the knower   2
of all fields, Scion of Bharata.
Knowledge of the field and its knower
I consider to be true knowing.

What this field is, and its nature,   3
its changes and how they arise,
and the powers of its knower—
listen now to my brief account.

Sages have often sung of this   4
in many different Vedic hymns,
in *sutras* concerning *Brahman*,
well-reasoned, irrefutable.

The great elements and selfhood,   5
intellect and the unmanifest,
all of the eleven senses,
the five fields of their perception,

Desire, loathing, pleasure, pain,   *6*
organic consciousness, and courage—
briefly put, all this is the field
and its so-called transformations.

Freedom from arrogance and deceit,   *7*
nonviolence, patience, rectitude,
respect for teachers, purity,
stability, and self-restraint,

An aversion to sense-objects,   *8*
absence of all *ahamkara*,
keeping in mind the misery
of birth, disease, old age, and death;

Nonattachment, never clinging   *9*
to one's family, home, and so forth,
and constant equanimity
when outcomes are desired or not;

Undeviating devotion   *10*
toward Me and to *Yoga* only,
often going on retreats alone
and disdaining social contact;

Constant awareness of the Spirit,   *11*
focus on truth and wisdom's goal—
all this is proclaimed as knowledge.
Ignorance is the opposite.

I will now say what must be known   *12*
to attain immortality,
beginningless, supreme *Brahman*,
neither being nor nonbeing.

Its hands and feet are everywhere,   *13*
everywhere eyes, heads, and faces,

ears that hear the entire world,
it stands pervading everything.

Manifest to all the senses   *14*
and yet free from all the senses,
unattached but all maintaining,
free from but enjoying *gunas*;

Outside and inside of beings,   *15*
those that move and those unmoving,
too subtle to be comprehended,
far away yet intimate.

Undivided, yet remaining   *16*
as if divided in all beings,
to be known as sustaining them,
devouring and creating them.

This is also the light of lights,   *17*
said to be beyond all darkness,
knowledge and the goal of knowledge,
seated in the hearts of all.

This is the field, knowledge of it,   *18*
and what must be known, briefly put.
Understanding this, My votary
comes close to My state of being.

Know too that matter and spirit   *19*
are also both beginningless,
and that the field in all its modes,
and the *gunas*, arise from matter.

Matter is said to be the cause   *20*
and the instrument of action.
Spirit is said to be the cause
of experiencing pain and pleasure.

Spirit, embedded in matter,   *21*
feels the *gunas* born of matter.
Attachment to the *gunas* causes
its birth in good and evil wombs.

That which witnesses and consents,   *22*
supports and experiences,
is called great Lord and highest Self,
supreme Spirit in the body.

One who knows spirit in this way,   *23*
and knows matter and the *gunas*,
in whatever state he might exist,
that one will not be born again.

Through meditation on the self   *24*
some perceive the Self in the self;
others through practicing *Samkhya*;
and others through *Karma Yoga*.

Some, however, not knowing this,   *25*
worship as they hear from others,
and they also can transcend death,
devoted to what they have heard.

Every being that is born,   *26*
whether standing still or moving,
comes from the union of the field
and the field's knower, Arjuna.

The one who sees the highest Lord   *27*
existing alike in all beings,
not perishing when they perish,
that is the one who truly sees.

Seeing the same Lord everywhere,   *28*
established everywhere he looks,

he does not injure Self with self
and goes on to the highest goal.

The one who sees that all actions   *29*
are performed by matter alone,
and so the Self is not the doer,
that is the one who sees indeed.

Perceiving Being's various states   *30*
as resting steady in the One
and spreading out from That alone,
one will then attain to *Brahman*.

Without beginning or qualities   *31*
the Supreme Self cannot perish.
Even though it is embodied,
it neither acts nor is befouled.

As the all-pervading ether,   *32*
being subtle, is not tainted,
so the Self, even when embodied,
never can itself be tainted.

As the sun alone illumines   *33*
this entire world, so also
the Lord of the field illumines
the entire field, O Arjuna.

Those who understand the difference   *34*
between the field and its knower,
and know beings' release from matter,
they go beyond, to the Supreme."

Chapter Fourteen

The Blessed Lord spoke:

"I will now go on to declare 1
the highest of all knowledges,
acquiring which all the sages
have attained utmost perfection.

Taking refuge in this knowledge, 2
attaining identity with Me,
they are not born even at creation
and do not tremble when all dissolves.

Great *Brahman* is for Me the womb 3
in which I place the embryo.
The origin of all beings
arises there, O Arjuna.

Whatever forms, Son of Kunti, 4
issue forth from any womb,
all have great *Brahman* as their womb,
and I am their seeding father.

Sattva, rajas, tamas—gunas 5
material nature has produced—
bind down *Atman* in the body,
though it is imperishable.

Of these, *sattva*, pure, untainted, 6
luminous, free from malady,
binds by attachment to happiness
and to knowledge, O Sinless One.

Know that *rajas* is marked by passion 7
that arises from desire.
This binds down embodied *Atman*
by attachment to activity.

Tamas is born of ignorance, 8
confusing all embodied beings,
binding them down with laziness
and torpor, Scion of Bharata.

Sattva, then, causes attachment 9
to happiness; *rajas* to action;
and *tamas*, obscuring knowledge,
causes attachment to indolence.

Sattva arises by subduing 10
rajas and *tamas*; *rajas* by subduing
sattva and *tamas*; and *tamas* by
subduing *sattva* and *rajas*.

When through all the body's portals 11
the light of wisdom starts to shine,
that is when it should be known
sattva has become dominant.

Avarice and activity, 12
restlessness and desire
arise in the ascendancy
of *rajas*, Bull of the Bharatas.

Gloominess, lack of exertion, 13
negligence, and confusion
arise in the ascendancy
of *tamas*, O Scion of Kuru.

If an embodied being dies 14
when *sattva* is predominant,

it goes to the pure, stainless worlds
of those with the highest wisdom.

One who dies in *rajas* is born   15
among those attached to action.
Dying while *tamas* is ascendant,
one is reborn from deluded wombs.

They say the fruit of good action   16
is *sattvic* without any stain.
The fruit of *rajas* is suffering,
the fruit of *tamas* ignorance.

From *sattva* arises knowledge,   17
and from *rajas* avarice;
sloth and delusion come from *tamas*
as does ignorance as well.

Those established in *sattva* rise;   18
the *rajasic* stay in the middle;
to the lowest state of *gunas*
far below go the *tamasic*.

When the seer perceives the doers   19
as none other than the *gunas*
and also knows what is higher,
he comes to attain My being.

Going beyond these three *gunas*,   20
which produce the body, freed from
the pain of birth, old age, and death,
Atman attains immortality."

Then Arjuna asked:

"One gone beyond these three *gunas*,   21
by what marks is he recognized?

How does he act? And how, Krishna,
does he transcend these three *gunas?*"

The Blessed Lord answered:

"He neither hates nor desires   22
either the presence or the absence
of brightness or activity
or of delusion, Son of Pandu.

Seated apart, dispassionate,   23
undisturbed by the *gunas*,
calmly watching *gunas* working,
standing firm, never wavering,

Self-contained, to whom pain and pleasure,   24
a clod, a stone, a lump of gold,
loved, and unloved are all equal,
steadfast whether blamed or praised,

The same in honor and disgrace,   25
impartial to friend and enemy,
renouncing all undertakings—
he is said to transcend the *gunas*.

And one who serves Me steadily   26
by practicing *Bhakti Yoga*
and transcendence of the *gunas*
soon will be absorbed in *Brahman*.

I am indeed the abode of *Brahman*,   27
of the immortal and the eternal,
and of everlasting *dharma*,
and of bliss that is absolute."

Chapter Fifteen

Then the Blessed Lord said:

"The eternal *ashvatta* tree,   *1*
with roots above, branches below,
has leaves that are the sacred hymns.
Who knows this tree knows the *Vedas*.

Its branches spread widely below and above,   *2*
    nourished by the *gunas*. Its sprouts can be sensed,
and its roots also stretch downward far below,
    engendering action in the human world.

The form of this tree cannot be perceived here,   *3*
    not its end, beginning, nor continuance.
Having cut this *ashvatta* tree off at the root
    with the strong, sharp ax of nonattachment,

One must then seek as the final goal that place   *4*
    from which, having once arrived, no one returns.
It is in that primal Spirit I take refuge,
    where the primeval energy first streamed forth.

Prideless, clear, evils of attachment conquered,   *5*
    in *Atman* constantly, desires averted,
free from duality of pleasure and pain,
    the undeluded go to that eternal place.

Neither the sun, nor the moon,   *6*
nor does fire illumine that place,
to which having gone none return.
That place is My supreme abode.

When a mere fraction of Myself 7
becomes a soul in the living world,
it draws to itself the sixth sense, mind,
and the others in material nature.

When the Lord acquires a body 8
and when too He leaves it behind,
He takes the senses along with Him
like wind bearing perfume away.

With hearing, sight, touch, taste, and smell 9
at His command, as well as mind,
the Lord as an incarnate soul
enjoys the objects of the senses.

When departing or remaining 10
or while enjoying with the *gunas*,
He is not seen by the deluded
but only by those with wisdom's eye.

Yogins strive and see the Lord 11
situated in the *Atman*,
but mindless, unperfected souls,
though they may strive, do not see Him.

The sun's brilliance that illumines 12
every corner of the universe
and is in the moon and in fire—
know the brilliance belongs to Me.

Alighting on earth I support 13
all beings with My energy,
and I cause all the plants to thrive,
becoming juicy-savored *soma*.

Entering all breathing bodies 14
I become their digestive fire.

With the inbreath and the outbreath
I digest the four kinds of food.

And I have entered the heart of all beings.   *15*
    Memory, knowledge, and their loss come from Me.
I am all there is to know in the *Vedas*;
    I made the *Vedanta*, am the *Vedas'* knower.

There are two spirits in the world,   *16*
one transient and one eternal.
All beings are the transient.
The unchanging is called the eternal.

But there is another higher spirit   *17*
that is called the Supreme *Atman*,
who going into the three worlds
supports them as their eternal Lord.

Since I transcend the transient,   *18*
am higher than the transient,
I am known as the Supreme Spirit
in the world and in the *Vedas*.

Those who know without delusion   *19*
that I am the Supreme Spirit
know everything and worship Me
with all their being, Arjuna.

This most secret of all doctrines   *20*
I have thus taught. Awakened to it,
one would be awakened truly,
all duties fulfilled, Arjuna."

Chapter Sixteen

The Blessed Lord spoke:

"Being fearless and pure of heart,
persevering in *Jnana Yoga*,
charity, restraint, and sacrifice,
study, ardor, and uprightness,

1

Nonviolence, non-calumny,
calmness, truth, renunciation,
compassion, freedom from desire,
kindness, modesty, steadiness,

2

Power, patience, strength, purity,
freedom from malice and from pride—
these are the traits of those destined
to be divine, O Arjuna.

3

Hypocrisy, arrogance, deceit,
anger, harshness, and ignorance—
these are the traits of those destined
to be demonic, O Arjuna.

4

Divine destiny liberates,
demonic destiny imprisons.
Do not worry! You are destined
to be divine, O Arjuna.

5

So in this world there are two kinds
of created beings. The divine
has just been thoroughly explained.
Now hear from Me the demonic.

6

Demonic beings do not know   *7*
when to act and when not to act.
Purity is not found in them,
nor is truth or good behavior.

They say that the world is not real,   *8*
has no foundation, has no God,
that God has not produced the world.
What then? The world is caused by lust.

Holding this view, these lost souls,   *9*
men of little intelligence,
evil actors, come forth, enemies
intent on this world's destruction.

Insatiable in their desires,   *10*
hypocritical and arrogant,
holding false ideas, deluded,
they proceed with impure purpose.

Clinging to immense anxiety   *11*
that ends when they dissolve in death;
fulfilling desire their highest goal,
convinced that this is all there is;

Bound by a hundred snares of hope,   *12*
devoted to desire and anger,
they strive to gratify desire
with hoards of wealth unjustly gained.

'This is what I obtained today;   *13*
I will gratify this desire;
this is now mine, and that also
will be added to my riches;

That enemy has been killed by me,   *14*
and I will kill others as well;

I am a lord, and I enjoy
success, power, and happiness;

I am wealthy and highborn.   *15*
Who else is my equal? I will
offer sacrifice, donate, rejoice.'
This is how they are deluded.

Carried away by many dreams,   *16*
trapped in a net of delusion,
living to fulfill their desires,
they fall into a hell most foul.

Self-centered, stubborn, arrogant   *17*
with pride of wealth, they sacrifice
in name only, hypocritically,
not according to precedent.

Egotistic and insolent,   *18*
attached to force, desire, anger,
out of envy they despise Me
in their own and others' bodies.

They hate, they are cruel, they are vile   *19*
and vicious men. I am always
hurling them into demons' wombs
in cycles of transmigrations.

Entering the wombs of demons,   *20*
deluded in birth after birth,
and never, Arjuna, reaching Me,
they go to the worst place of all.

There is a triple gate to hell   *21*
that is destructive of the self:
these are desire, greed, and anger.
Therefore one should renounce all three.

If when released, Son of Kunti,   22
from this triple *tamasic* gate
one does what is best for the Self,
then he reaches the highest goal.

One who ignores scriptural rules   23
and acts according to desire
never will attain perfection,
nor happiness, nor the highest goal.

So let scripture set your standard   24
for what may and may not be done.
Knowing what the scriptures prescribe
should guide your actions in this world."

Chapter Seventeen

Arjuna then asked:

"Those who cast the scriptures aside   *1*
but still sacrifice, filled with faith,
what would be their standing, Krishna?
Sattvic, rajasic, or *tamasic?*"

The Blessed Lord said:

"The faith of embodied beings   *2*
is of three kinds, innate in them:
either *sattvic* or *rajasic*
or *tamasic.* Now hear of this.

Faith aligns with the true nature   *3*
of every being, Arjuna.
A person is made of his faith.
Whichever faith he has, he is.

Sattvic people worship the gods;   *4*
rajasic, spirits and demons;
the others, *tamasic,* worship
ghosts and hordes of nature spirits.

Those who suffer austerities   *5*
not prescribed in the scriptures,
hypocritical, egoistic,
with desire, force, and passion,

Mindlessly torturing the body's   *6*
multitudinous elements,
and therefore Me in the body—
see their intent as demonic.

Peoples' preferences for food　　　　　　　　*7*
are also triple, as are gifts,
sacrifices, and austerities.
Hear now how all these differ.

Foods that promote longevity,　　　　　　　　*8*
strength, health, virtue, satisfaction,
and are tasty, smooth, digestible—
these foods are prized by the *sattvic*.

Foods that are bitter, sour, salty,　　　　　　*9*
hot and spicy, dry and burning,
are desired by the *rajasic*.
They cause misery and sickness.

Putrid, rotten, leftover food,　　　　　　　　*10*
tasteless, foul, rejected garbage,
not suitable for sacrifice,
is preferred by the *tamasic*.

Sacrifice observing scripture　　　　　　　　*11*
without desire for its fruits,
the mind fixed only on the thought
'this must be offered'—that is *sattvic*.

But sacrifice that is offered　　　　　　　　*12*
for the hypocritical purpose
of its fruit, such a sacrifice
understand to be *rajasic*.

A sacrifice without scripture,　　　　　　　　*13*
lacking mantras, no food offered,
the fee unpaid, devoid of faith,
is regarded as *tamasic*.

Worshipping gods, the twice-born, sages,　　　*14*
teachers too; purity, virtue,

celibacy, and nonviolence
are called bodily austerities.

Language that is not distressing   15
but truthful, pleasing, beneficial,
and practice reciting sacred texts,
these are vocal austerities.

Mental calmness, benevolence,   16
keeping silence, self-restraint,
purity of being also,
these are mental austerities.

These three austerities, practiced   17
with utmost faith by men who are
steadfast and not desiring fruits,
are considered to be *sattvic*.

But if practiced insincerely   18
for honor, reverence, or respect,
austerity is called *rajasic*,
unsteady and impermanent.

Austerity that is performed   19
with delusions of self-torture
or to destroy another
is declared to be *tamasic*.

A gift with just the thought 'giving,'   20
not repaying, to someone worthy
and at the proper time and place,
such a gift is seen as *sattvic*.

A gift, however, that is given   21
as recompense, and grudgingly,
or with the aim of some profit,
is regarded as *rajasic*.

A gift at the wrong place and time,   22
given to an unworthy person,
without respect or with contempt,
is declared to be *tamasic*.

Om tat sat. This three-word mantra   23
signifies and summons *Brahman*.
This mantra of old created
brahmins, *Vedas*, and sacrifices.

So when beginning sacrifice,   24
acts of giving, austerities,
expounders of *Brahman* utter '*Om*'
as prescribed in Vedic scriptures.

Saying '*tat*' without thought of fruit,   25
various acts of sacrifice,
of giving and austerity,
are done by those who seek release.

'*Sat*' is used in its meanings   26
of goodness and reality.
The word '*sat*' is also used
for praiseworthy acts, Arjuna.

Steadfastness in austerity,   27
in sacrifice and in giving
and in any related action,
is likewise referred to as '*sat*.'

Oblations and austerities   28
that are performed with lack of faith
are called '*asat*,' Son of Pritha,
and are void here and hereafter."

Chapter Eighteen

Arjuna then said:

"I wish to know, Mighty Armed One, *1*
exactly what renunciation is
and what is meant by abandonment,
each of them, Slayer of Keshin."

The Blessed Lord spoke:

"By renunciation the sages mean *2*
forsaking desire-driven actions.
Relinquishing all fruits of action
is what they call abandonment.

Some sages say that all action *3*
is evil and should be renounced.
Sacrifice, giving, austerity
should not be renounced, others say.

Now listen to what I conclude *4*
concerning this, O Arjuna.
Renunciation is of three kinds,
O Best of the Bharatas.

Sacrifice, giving, austerity *5*
must be performed, not renounced.
Sacrifice, giving, austerity
purify the minds of the wise.

But these actions must be performed *6*
while renouncing all attachment
to their fruits. This, Son of Pritha,
is without doubt my deep belief.

And renunciation is not proper   *7*
when actions are obligatory.
Such deluded renunciation
is declared to be *tamasic*.

Not acting because it is hard   *8*
or out of fear of suffering
is *rajasic*. One does not obtain
fruit from such renunciation.

Performing an ordained action   *9*
with discipline, O Arjuna,
and no attachment to its fruit,
that is *sattvic* renunciation.

The wise man, his doubt severed,   *10*
the renunciant, filled with goodness,
does not hate displeasing action,
nor is attached to pleasant action.

Embodied beings are not able   *11*
to forgo action entirely.
But one who forgoes action's fruits
is said to be a renunciant.

The fruits of action are threefold   *12*
for non-renunciants when they die:
unpleasant, pleasant, and a mixture.
But for renunciants none at all.

And now, Mighty Armed Arjuna,   *13*
learn from Me of the five factors,
as declared in *Samkhya* doctrine,
for accomplishing all actions.

First the basis, second the agent,   *14*
third, the various kinds of organs,

fourth, the different kinds of motions,
fifth, the relevant deities.

Whatever action one performs   15
whether with body, speech, or mind,
and whether it is right or wrong,
these five are the causal factors.

This being so, whoever sees   16
himself alone as the agent
has imperfect understanding
and does not really see, the fool.

One who is not egocentric,   17
whose intellect is untainted,
even though he kills these people,
he does not kill, and is not bound.

Knowledge, the known, and the knower   18
are the threefold drivers of action.
The means, the act, and the agent
are action's three constituents.

Knowledge, action, and the agent   19
are of three kinds, each distinguished
by the *gunas*. Learn these also,
as they are declared in *Samkhya*.

The knowledge by which one sees   20
a single being in all creatures,
undivided and eternal,
know that knowledge to be *sattvic*.

But the knowledge by which one sees   21
different beings of various kinds
in all the creatures of the world,
see that knowledge as *rajasic*.

And the knowledge that is attached   22
to one paltry deed as being all,
without reason or real purpose,
that knowledge is called *tamasic*.

Restrained action free from clinging,   23
done without desire or hatred
and with no yearning for its fruit,
such an action is called *sattvic*.

Action done to attain desires,   24
or done out of selfishness,
or performed with too much effort
is declared to be *rajasic*.

Deluded action that ignores   25
consequences, loss, hurting others,
and one's own capability
is spoken of as *tamasic*.

Free from clinging and self-interest,   26
steadfast, resolved, and unperturbed
either by success or failure,
such an agent is called *sattvic*.

Passionate, craving action's fruits,   27
greedy, violent, and impure,
beset both by joy and sorrow,
such an agent is *rajasic*.

Undisciplined, vulgar, stubborn,   28
wicked, idle, and deceitful,
desperate and always dawdling,
such an agent is *tamasic*.

Hear now the threefold distinction   29
of intellect and steadfastness

set forth in reference to the *gunas*,
one by one, leaving nothing out.

Knowing action and inaction,   *30*
what to fear and what not to fear,
knowing bondage and liberation,
that is a *sattvic* intellect.

An intellect incapable   *31*
of distinguishing right from wrong,
what is duty from what is not,
is *rajasic*, Son of Pritha.

An intellect that, cloaked in darkness,   *32*
is convinced what is wrong is right
and that all things are perverted,
is *tamasic*, Son of Pritha.

The steadfastness that through *Yoga*   *33*
holds the functions of the senses,
the mind and breath without swerving,
is called *sattvic*, Son of Pritha.

The steadfastness with which one holds   *34*
on to duty, wealth, and pleasure
with attachment, desiring fruit,
is called *rajasic*, Arjuna.

The steadfastness with which the dull   *35*
do not give up sleep, fear, sorrow,
lethargy, and self-importance,
is called *tamasic*, Arjuna.

And now, Bull of the Bharatas,   *36*
learn from Me the threefold happiness
enjoyed through practice, and by which
one comes to the end of suffering.

Happiness at first like poison
but then transformed into nectar,
born from one's own luminous mind,
is considered to be *sattvic*.

37

First like nectar through the contact
of the senses with their objects,
but then transformed into poison,
that happiness is called *rajasic*.

38

That happiness, which both at first
and afterward deludes the self,
born of sleep, sloth, and confusion,
is declared to be *tamasic*.

39

There is no being, either on earth
or even in heaven among the gods,
that can exist at all without
these three *gunas* born from matter.

40

All the duties of the *brahmins*,
the *kshatriyas*, the *vaishyas*,
and the *shudras* are apportioned
according to their innate *gunas*.

41

Calmness, restraint, austerity,
honesty, patience, purity,
knowledge, faith, and discernment
are the *brahmins*' natural duties.

42

Heroic courage, majesty,
expertise, staunchness in battle,
generosity, lordliness,
are the *kshatriyas*' natural duties.

43

Plowing, cowherding, and trade
are the *vaishyas*' innate duties.

44

Everything to do with service
is the *shudras'* natural duty.

Contented with his own duties, 45
a man attains full perfection.
Listen now how one contented
with his duties finds perfection.

Worshipping through his own duty 46
the origin of all beings
who pervades the entire universe
is how man attains perfection.

Better one's own duty poorly 47
than another's well performed.
Performing one's inborn duty,
a person never incurs guilt.

Never abandon inborn duty 48
even when faulty, Arjuna.
All new actions are enveloped
with faultiness, as fire by smoke.

With intellect always unattached, 49
with self conquered, desire dispelled,
one attains by renunciation
perfect, unexcelled nonaction.

Learn from Me briefly, Arjuna, 50
how having attained perfection
one also attains to *Brahman*,
the consummate state of wisdom.

Conjoined with a pure intellect, 51
firmly in control of the self,
abandoning all the senses,
rejecting both desire and hatred,

Dwelling alone, eating lightly,   52
controlling speech, body, and mind,
devoted to *Dhyana Yoga*,
taking refuge in dispassion,

Relinquishing egoism,   53
force, pride, desire, anger,
and possessions; selfless, tranquil,
one is fit to unite with *Brahman*.

Absorbed in *Brahman*, self serene,   54
without sorrow or desire,
impartial to all, one attains
devotion to Me that is supreme.

Devoted to Me, one comes to know   55
how great and who I really am.
Knowing Me in reality,
immediately one enters Me.

And, performing every action   56
always with reliance on Me,
from My grace one attains the eternal
and imperishable abode.

Concentrating on renouncing   57
all action in Me as supreme,
relying on *Buddhi Yoga*,
constantly keep your thoughts on Me.

Thinking of Me you will transcend   58
every obstacle by My grace.
But if out of egoism
you do not listen, then you perish.

If you retreat into your ego   59
and say to yourself, 'I will not fight,'

your resolve will prove untrue.
Nature itself will force your hand.

Bound by your *karma*, Arjuna,   60
that is born from your own nature,
you will do what in delusion
is contrary to your wishes.

The Lord abides deep in the hearts   61
of all beings, O Arjuna,
making them move by illusion,
like puppets mounted on a machine.

Go to Him alone, your refuge,   62
with all your being, Bharata!
By His grace you will attain
supreme peace in eternity.

This knowledge that I've expounded   63
is the secret of all secrets.
Consider it in its entirety,
and then do just as you desire.

Hear again My most secret word   64
and My ultimate utterance.
You are assuredly loved by Me,
and so I will speak for your good.

Worship Me with devotion,   65
sacrifice to Me, bow to Me.
So shall you truly come to Me,
I avow, for you are dear to Me.

Abandoning all your duties,   66
take refuge in Me alone.
I will free you from all evils;
you should never grieve or sorrow.

Always keep this from those without   67
austere practice and devotion,
from those who do not wish to listen,
and from those who speak ill of Me.

Whoever sets forth this highest,   68
secret teaching to My votaries,
and has worshipped Me devoutly,
will come to Me without a doubt.

And no one among men will do   69
more pleasing work for Me than he;
and no other upon this earth
will be to Me more beloved.

Whoever studies and recites   70
this sacred dialogue of ours,
will have cherished Me, I avow,
with the sacrifice of wisdom.

Even one who only hears it,   71
full of faith and without scoffing,
will be freed in the happy worlds
of people who have acted purely.

Have you now heard this with your mind   72
in one-pointed concentration?
Have your ignorance and delusion
been destroyed, O Son of Pritha?"

Arjuna answered:

"My delusion is gone; I have gained   73
wisdom through Your grace, O Krishna,
and am standing with doubt dispelled.
I will carry out Your orders."

Then Sanjaya said:

"Thus I have heard from Lord Krishna 74
and the great-souled Son of Pritha—
this miraculous dialogue
that caused my hair to stand on end.

By Vyasa's grace I have heard 75
this supreme and secret *Yoga*
that Krishna, the Lord of *Yoga*
Himself, divulged before my eyes.

O King, each time I remember 76
this miraculous dialogue
between Arjuna and Krishna,
I rejoice again and again.

And each time that I remember 77
Krishna's most astonishing form,
I am overcome with wonder
and I rejoice anew, O King.

Wherever there is the Lord of *Yoga*, 78
wherever Arjuna, the archer,
there will be splendor, victory,
wealth, and goodness, I am certain."

AFTERWORD:
KRISHNA ON MODERN
FIELDS OF BATTLE

In the first verse of the *Bhagavad Gita*, the blind king Dhritarashtra asks his courtier Sanjaya, who has been granted divine vision, what has happened on Kurukshetra, the "field of *dharma*." The place of battle is indeed an arena of *dharma*, that key Sanskrit term that denotes law, duty, righteous conduct, and much more. With its ultimate stakes of life and death, war poses to its warriors profound questions of honor, loyalty, and ethical choice. So often war leaves its surviving warriors, even the so-called victors, with deep wounds, and not only physical ones. Grief, trauma, guilt, and moral injury may have lingering, debilitating effects for years after, just as they did for the victorious Pandavas. It is no accident that Krishna's teachings at Kurukshetra, with their deep reflections arising from Arjuna's grief and confusion at the violence to come, have often found eager listeners on modern fields of battle.

The *Mahabharata* describes two immense armies facing one another across an immense field, preparing for direct person-to-person violent combat—a classic scene of battle. But this is not the only kind of battlefield. In modern times, places of combat can be diffuse and impersonal, and they can often be far removed from direct physical violence. Yet here too the moral issues are just as imposing, and the traumas of battle can be just as paralyzing. And here too the teachings of the *Bhagavad Gita* can resonate for those engaged in modern battle. In this Afterword we consider three figures engaged in the great conflicts of the mid-twentieth century: the Indian leader of the struggle for Indian independence, Mohandas Gandhi; the American physicist and scientific director of the Manhattan Project at Los Alamos, J. Robert Oppenheimer; and the British novelist, pacifist, and exponent of a "perennial philosophy," Aldous Huxley. Each grappled with the *Bhagavad Gita*. Each read within his own situation, and each found in Krishna's complex teachings advice and reassurance that resonated with their own needs and their own objectives.

Gandhi, the *Gita*, and the Salt Campaign

At dawn on March 12, 1930, the seventy-two selected Marchers assembled in the Sabarmati ashram, just south of Ahmedabad in Gujarat, ready to set out on their campaign. All wore simple clothes of homespun white cotton. Some wore chappals, while others went barefoot. Their hands were empty, but each carried a backpack with a bedroll, a change of clothes, and a few other items. All were male, and most were young men between the ages of twenty and twenty-five. The oldest Marcher was the leader of the march, Mohandas Gandhi, age sixty.

In his brief remarks just before the Marchers set out, Gandhi portrayed this journey as a "life-and-death struggle, a holy war."[1] Indeed, the campaign had been planned just as meticulously as any military operation. Gandhi had personally selected for Marchers only those who had undergone rigid discipline and were firmly committed to the principles of the struggle. Gandhi and this elite group would march for twenty-four days, two hundred miles from Sabarmati to Dandi, on the shore of the Arabian Sea. With characteristic attention to detail, Gandhi set out austere guidelines for each of the day's meals. He specified that vegetables be boiled with no oil, spices, or chilies, and that the Marchers accept no sweets. Along the way they should halt at select villages to rest, spin, collect information, hold public assemblies, and give speeches. They would reach Dandi on April 5, and there, on the beach that Gandhi called the "battle-field of satyagraha," he and the Marchers would collect the natural salt found along the seashore. They fully expected to be arrested by the British colonial government before achieving their aim.

Gandhi repeatedly spoke of the Salt March in military terms, as a campaign, a struggle, a "battle of Right against Might." But it was certainly a most unusual offensive, not at all like the massive armies on the plains of Kurukshetra. The irony was not lost on those who observed it. Herbert Miller, an American sociologist who reported on the Salt March for *The Nation*, wrote: "This call to arms was perhaps the most remarkable call to war that has ever been made. The dominant notes were non-violence, non-hatred,

---

1. Mahatma Gandhi, *Collected Works of Mahatma Gandhi* (Delhi: Publications Division, Government of India, 1958–1984), vol. 43, p. 60.

self-discipline, and sacrifice, fearlessness and persistence to the end."[2] The seventy-two Marchers had been trained in the rigorous techniques of nonviolent *satyagraha* (literally, "holding fast to Truth"). The troops were unarmed, and they brought along only the barest provisions for their march. In their packs, according to Gandhi's directives, they carried not ammunition but diaries and copies of Gandhi's own translation of the *Bhagavad Gita*.[3] The objective of this elaborate campaign was the simplest of everyday commodities: salt.

At the ashram, Kasturba Gandhi applied a ceremonial *tilaka* to the forehead of her husband and placed on his shoulders a garland not of flowers but of khadi, homespun cotton. A friend gave Gandhi a staff of lacquered bamboo, which would become a common emblem in the iconography of Gandhi. Coconuts were broken, to bring good fortune to the March. Prayers were offered and devotional songs were sung. The Salt March was as much a religious pilgrimage as it was a military operation. At exactly 6:30 Gandhi consulted his watch and set out with his elite Marchers. The crowd of some 20,000 persons cried out "Victory to Mahatma Gandhi" as the procession set out. It was a most dramatic departure, and those who observed the start of this historic event compared it with other legendary departures.

> The scene reminded some of Rama's march on Lanka, others of the exodus of the Israelites under Moses, still others saw it as Krishna leaving Gokul or Rama leaving Ayodhya for fourteen years of exile in the forest. The most common comparison, however, was with the Buddha's great renunciation.[4]

Whatever the best historical analogy, Gandhi himself chose the *Bhagavad Gita* as the text that would accompany the Salt March. At the time, he viewed this work as "an infallible guide to conduct" and a "spiritual reference book." It is no accident that his own Gujarati translation of the *Bhagavad Gita* was published on March 12, 1930, the day the Marchers set out from Sabarmati.[5]

---

2. Herbert A. Miller, "Gandhi's Campaign Begins," *The Nation* 130 (April 23, 1930), p. 501.
3. Gandhi, *Collected Works*, vol. 42, p. 12.
4. Thomas Weber, *On the Salt March: The Historiography of Gandhi's March to Dandi* (New Delhi: HarperCollins Publishers, 1997), p. 138.
5. M. K. Gandhi, *An Autobiography: The Story of My Experiments with Truth* (Boston: Beacon Press, 1957), p. 265.

Gandhi found in the *Gita* a work of moral instruction that helped articulate his own conceptions of personal austerity and worldly engagement in the struggle for justice.

Leader of the largest and most sustained anti-colonial struggle of the twentieth century, Gandhi was renowned for his deep commitment to the principle of nonviolence. To many critics and observers, his selection of the *Bhagavad Gita* as a spiritual guide to conduct seemed to contradict this principle. After all, the instigating purpose of Krishna's teachings is to persuade Arjuna to fight, to engage in a battle of dreadful violence. Gandhi acknowledged that he did not derive his fundamental principle of *ahimsa* or nonviolence directly from the *Bhagavad Gita*. However, he argued, the true Kurukshetra was to be found not on a physical battlefield but within each of us, in our heart or conscience. The *Mahabharata* is an allegorical work, he proposed, in which the contending sides represent the "higher" and "baser" impulses within us. "Under the guise of physical warfare," he wrote in the introduction to his translation, the *Gita* and the *Mahabharata* "described the duel that perpetually went on in the hearts of mankind." Within this allegorical interpretation, he added, "Krishna is the Dweller within, ever whispering in a pure heart."

For Gandhi, Krishna's most profound instruction in the *Bhagavad Gita* lay in the renunciation of attachment to the fruits of action. Like Arjuna, Gandhi found himself inescapably engaged in the central struggle of his time. His path lay firmly in *Karma Yoga*. Renunciation of his social and political work was not an option for him. He accepted the premise that all action binds. He acknowledged the problem he faced, the same as that faced by Arjuna: how can one reconcile a life of active worldly engagement with the pursuit of liberation from bondage, the highest spiritual goal? Krishna's unique solution to this, Gandhi restated, is: "Do your allotted work, but renounce its fruits. Be detached and work. Have no desire for reward and work." This was the center around which Krishna wove all his teachings.

Gandhi recognized the difficulty in attaining this detachment-in-work, just as Arjuna did. It requires a "constant heart-churn," he observed. One must make a constant disciplined effort to practice the self-restraints that enable one to act without attachment. For Gandhi, the most succinct description of one who has achieved such mastery of the self is Krishna's account of the *sthitaprajna*, the person in whom wisdom stands firm. Gandhi did not claim to have achieved this state himself, but he did claim to have made forty years' unremitting endeavor fully to enforce the teachings of the *Gita* in his own life. He sought also to enforce Krishna's teachings on others around him. In the Sabermati ashram, where the Salt Marchers received their training, collective recitation of Krishna's description of the *sthitaprajna* was a regular feature of the evening prayer sessions. This would cultivate in them the qualities of nonviolence, non-hatred, self-discipline, sacrifice, fearlessness, and persistence (exactly as the reporter Herbert Miller had observed) needed to confront without violence or retaliation the violent beatings with police clubs and incarceration that likely faced them when they set out from the ashram toward Dandi.

Oppenheimer and the *Gita* at Los Alamos

Well before dawn on July 16, 1945, twenty or so people—soldiers, officers of the United States Army and Navy, physicists, and one reporter from the *New York Times*—assembled in the main control bunker, about twenty miles northwest of the location in the high New Mexican desert they called "Zero," site of the "Trinity" test. Zero was where the "gadget" had been assembled atop a one-hundred-foot steel tower. The "gadget" was the laconic term by which the physicists referred to a new, complex, and extraordinarily potent five-ton apparatus designed to create the world's first human-controlled atomic explosion.

Inside the bunker the mood was tense. The scientific director of the Manhattan Project, J. Robert Oppenheimer, was beyond calming. As the military officer Thomas Farrell recounted a few days later, Oppenheimer "grew tenser as the last seconds ticked off. He scarcely breathed. He held on to a post to steady himself."[6] For two and a half years, an isolated cadre of scientists led by Oppenheimer had worked frantically in utmost secrecy, under strict military supervision, to develop a new kind of bomb that could be used against the Axis powers Germany and Japan. In the modern conditions of twentieth-century war, scientific laboratories had also become fields of battle, and the Manhattan physicists had labored with the deep fear, at

---

6. Cynthia C. Kelly, *The Manhattan Project: The Birth of the Atomic Bomb in the Words of Its Creators, Eyewitnesses, and Historians* (New York: Black Dog & Leventhal Publishers, 2007), p. 295.

least until the autumn of 1944, that German scientists might develop the new weapon before the Allies. If successful, the scientists realized, the gadget would radically alter the nature of war. Or perhaps it would alter the world itself. The evening before the detonation, Enrico Fermi had taken wagers from other scientists on whether the explosion would ignite the atmosphere, and if so, whether it would destroy just New Mexico, or the entire world. Oppenheimer and the others now awaited the detonation of the gadget.

As the countdown headed toward the 5:30 discharge, the personnel inside and outside the bunker followed the instructions of the military director, General Leslie R. Groves. They lay face down, with heads away from the explosion site. They closed their eyes and shielded them with their arms. They were told not to look up until after the initial flash of light, and only then to roll over and look through smoked welder's glass toward the blast.

The explosion was, by all accounts, extraordinary. Even at twenty miles distance, the burst of light was beyond all comparison, greater (Groves noted) "than any human had ever experienced":

> For a fraction of a second the light in that bell-shaped fire mass was greater than any ever produced before on earth. Its intensity was such that it could have been seen from another planet. The temperature at its center was four times that at the center of the sun and more than 10,000 times that at the sun's surface. The pressure, caving in the ground beneath, was over 100 billion atmospheres, the most ever to occur at the earth's surface.[7]

The reporter on the scene, William L. Laurence, gave a more vivid descriptive account.

> Up it went, a great ball of fire about a mile in diameter, changing colors as it kept shooting upward, from deep purple to orange, expanding, growing bigger, rising as it was expanding, an elemental force freed from its bonds after being chained for billions of years. For a fleeting instant the color was unearthly green, such as one sees only in the corona of the sun during a total eclipse. It was as though the earth had opened and the skies had split.[8]

---

7. Lansing Lamont, *Day of Trinity* (New York: Atheneum, 1965), pp. 235–36.
8. Ferenc Morton Szasz, *The Day the Sun Rose Twice: The Story of the Trinity Nuclear Explosion, July 16, 1945* (Albuquerque: University of New Mexico Press, 1984), p. 89.

The blast may have had an amazing, uncanny beauty, but it also created a wave of death. Every living thing within a mile radius of the Trinity site—squirrels, lizards, rattlesnakes, yucca plants, grass, and ants—was annihilated.

Faced with an unprecedented man-made phenomenon, eyewitnesses and other observers struggled to find apt comparisons. Some local residents who just happened to be in the area speculated that the sun had just come up and then suddenly gone down again. Others, more aware of the reason behind the event, reached for similes to the Judeo-Christian Bible. As reporter Laurence put it, "One felt as though he had been privileged to witness the Birth of the World—to be present at the moment of Creation when the Lord said: 'Let There Be Light.'"[9] But as the man who had directed the project, Oppenheimer looked elsewhere for a more ambiguous metaphor. At that moment, the culmination of all his efforts, he thought of a passage from the *Bhagavad Gita*.

> If the radiance of a thousand suns
> Were to burst at once into the sky,
> That would be like the splendor
>   of the Mighty One . . .
> I am become Death
> The shatterer of worlds.[10]

Oppenheimer had studied Sanskrit and read the text in its original language as a young professor at Berkeley a decade before his work at Los Alamos, and would speak of it often throughout his career. In 1932 he cited the *Gita* in letters to his younger brother Frank, urging on him the importance of *Yoga* or discipline. In April 1945, speaking to an impromptu assembly at Los Alamos mourning the death of Franklin Delano Roosevelt, Oppenheimer quoted Krishna's statement "Man is a creature whose substance is faith. What his faith is, he is." And he kept a worn pink copy of the work in "an honored place on the bookshelf closest to his desk."[11] In 1963, when the *Christian Century* asked Oppenheimer for a list of ten books that had shaped his outlook, he listed the *Bhagavad Gita* second. Only Baudelaire topped Krishna.

---

9. Szasz, *Day the Sun Rose Twice*, p. 89.

10. *Bhagavad Gita* 11.12 and 11.32 (evidently Oppenheimer's own translation).

11. Richard Rhodes, *The Making of the Atomic Bomb* (New York: Simon & Schuster, 1986), p. 662.

In Arjuna's vision of the god Krishna's all-encompassing Supernal Form on the eve of battle, Oppenheimer found at this moment an image of compelling awe and fearsomeness that could match the power he had helped unleash upon the world. In quoting the *Bhagavad Gita*, Oppenheimer also alluded to a theme to which he would often return in the aftermath of war. After the atomic destruction of Hiroshima and Nagasaki, there were intense debates over the wartime decision to deploy the bomb against urban targets. Fermi's wager was partly borne out. If the detonation at Los Alamos did not destroy the world, the atomic bomb certainly did alter the nature of the post-war world. As scientific director of the bomb's development, Oppenheimer played a central role in many of these debates, both as participant and target. Critics on the right attacked him for his alleged ties to Communist front organizations before the war, while left-wing critics berated him for complicity or support in the deployment of the bomb. Many of Oppenheimer's scientific colleagues had argued vociferously during the war against the use of the bomb on any civilian target and continued their efforts after the war to control the development of atomic weaponry.

Oppenheimer's response to these criticisms was complex and ambivalent, and he certainly experienced personal remorse. He spoke of having "blood on his hands." But he often drew on the *Bhagavad Gita* and its notion of *dharma* as a means of overcoming this deep sense of stain.

Krishna directs Arjuna to engage in battle as a trained member of the Kshatriya class, as part of his class duty or *dharma*. Oppenheimer envisioned his own social duty in terms of his professional education and expertise as a physicist, a scientist. As scientific director, he had exercised his scientific duty to the best of his ability. But as a scientist, he claimed, he did not have the information, the training, or the social responsibility to make political decisions about the ultimate use of the weapon. That was the *dharma* of others, the statesmen and political leaders elected to take on those awesome responsibilities. Krishna's teachings about duty could help Oppenheimer gain a perspective by which he could understand his own conduct as the *dharma* of a professional scientist enlisted in a wartime task. And insofar as he could gain detachment from the fruits of his own actions, he sought to overcome his post-war grief over the terrible wartime destruction in which he had played such a significant role.

Huxley, the *Gita*, and Perennial Philosophy

In mid-1944, American and British forces fought their way ashore on Normandy beaches, and their Russian allies mounted a massive counterattack on German forces in Belarus. In Poona, India, Mohandas Gandhi was in jail, spinning and reading the *Bhagavad Gita*, for his actions in leading the culminating anti-colonial campaign called "Quit India." J. Robert Oppenheimer was organizing the chemists, physicists, and engineers assembled in the New Mexican desert at Los Alamos. And at Llano, in the Mojave Desert outside Los Angeles, the British émigré intellectual Aldous Huxley was beginning work on a new book project.

Huxley wrote in April that year that he was finally undertaking an anthology "devoted to what has been called the Perennial Philosophy, the Highest Common Factor underlying all the great religious and metaphysical systems of the world."[12] This was not escapism. Huxley viewed this work as his response to the war raging throughout the world. He envisioned it as a foundation for restoring a post-war order.

> Seeing that it is perfectly obvious that we shall never have more than a temporary truce until most men accept a common *weltanschauung*, it would seem to be useful and timely to produce such a book, showing precisely what the best and most intelligent human beings have in fact agreed upon during the last three thousand years or so.[13]

He completed the anthology entitled *The Perennial Philosophy* in 1945, just as the World War was exploding to a close.

A prolific and successful British writer, Huxley emigrated to the United States in 1937. As a committed pacifist, he joined with another British intellectual, Gerald Heard, lecturing throughout the United States to advocate peace. At the completion of their tour, he settled in Los Angeles, where he—along with Heard and another immigrant British writer, Christopher Isherwood—came into contact with two Indian religious teachers: the former theosophist and independent philosopher Jaddu Krishnamurti, and the head of the Vedanta Center of Southern California, Swami Prabhavananda.

---

12. Huxley to Cass Canfield, April 9, 1944, in Grover Smith, *Letters of Aldous Huxley*, (New York: Harper & Row, 1969), p. 502.
13. Ibid.

Previously Huxley had mocked the "wisdom of the east." On a lengthy tour of British India in 1925–1926, he had disdained Indian spirituality as "the primal curse of India and the cause of all her misfortunes."[14] But by the early 1940s, with his earlier idealistic hopes for peace and international cooperation crushed by the war in Europe, Huxley's conversations with these erudite Indian thinkers led him to change dramatically and to consider mystical religion to be "the sole hope of the world."[15]

Isherwood took initiation into the Vedanta community in 1940 and came to regard Swami Prabhavananda as his personal guru. Later he moved into the monastic wing of the Vedanta Center as a male monk and committed himself to a program of meditation and study under Prabhavananda's supervision. During the war years of 1942 to 1945, Isherwood and Prabhavananda collaborated on a new translation of the *Bhagavad Gita*, with Huxley's encouragement and help. But Huxley was put off by the devotional atmosphere around the Center. His path led in a different direction, one that *Gita* commentators would classify as *Jnana Yoga*. While Isherwood meditated and translated, Huxley read widely in all the world's spiritual traditions, and he began to see a great pattern. As he reported to Isherwood in June 1944, "it all falls together like the outline of a system—a kind of miniature Summa."[16]

Huxley derives the term "perennial philosophy" from the seventeenth-century German philosopher G. W. Leibniz, but the thing to which the term refers is, he avers, much more ancient and universal. The sources Huxley consulted in assembling his Summa ranged over 2,500 years and came from Hindu, Buddhist, Taoist, Jewish, Christian, and Islamic Sufi writings. This single system, he states, centers around a divine Reality that is substantial within the things and persons of the everyday world. But the nature of this Reality "cannot be directly and immediately apprehended except by those who have chosen to fulfill certain conditions."[17] Those who do gain a

---

14. Sybille Bedford, *Aldous Huxley: A Biography* (London: Chatto & Windus, 1973–1974), vol. I, p. 165.

15. Huxley to Mary Hutcheson, 1942, in Nicholas Murray, *Aldous Huxley: An English Intellectual* (London: Little, Brown, 2002), p. 344.

16. Huxley to Christopher Isherwood, June 13, 1944, unpublished letter in Papers of Christopher Isherwood, 1864–1997. Huntington Library manuscript archive, Pasadena, CA.

17. Aldous Huxley, *The Perennial Philosophy* (New York: Harper and Brothers, 1945), p. viii.

first-hand glimpse into this Reality, he says, are known as saints, prophets, sages, or enlightened beings. Huxley's project was to bring together the first-hand reports of the sages, organize them thematically, and link them together with his own interpretive commentary.

The *Bhagavad Gita* played a central part in Huxley's Summa. As he writes in his introduction to the translation of Prabhavananda and Isherwood, this work "is perhaps the most systematic scriptural statement of the Perennial Philosophy."[18] He goes on to emphasize the pertinence of the *Gita* and the philosophy it espouses to the current world situation of 1945: "To a world at war, a world that, because it lacks the intellectual and spiritual prerequisites to peace, can only hope to patch up some kind of precarious armed truce, it stands pointing, clearly and unmistakably, to the road of escape from the self-imposed necessity of self-destruction."[19] Out of grief and despair, perhaps, could come some alternative to a precarious armed truce, some sort of new foundation for peace and international cooperation through a shared philosophy.

Huxley may have pitched his Summa at the highest level. He was not so much naïve about the prospects of the perennial philosophy becoming the basis of the new post-war order, so much as pessimistic about the alternative. He had set out, he wrote to Henry Miller, "a doctrine of which the modern world has chosen to be ignorant, preferring radios and four-motored bombers and salvation-through-organization, with the catastrophic consequences that we see all around us."[20] But at least one reviewer imagined its effects operating on the more intimate level of the individual veteran returning from the theater of war. Writing in *The New York Times Book Review*, Signe Toksvig described such a potential reader:

> A young American who had had a close look at what war was like, wrote home that, in regard to his plans for the future, he considered it at least as important to try and find out about God as to go into the insurance business. He also told his startled parents that he might carry out his search in a community of Quakers, a Franciscan monastery, a neo-Buddhistic monastery, and the Chicago Divinity

---

18. Aldous Huxley, "Introduction," in Swami Prabhavananda and Christopher Isherwood, *Bhagavad-gita: The Song of God* (Hollywood: Marel Rodd, 1944), p. 17.
19. Ibid.
20. Huxley to Henry Miller, 5 July 1945, in Smith, *Letters*, p. 529.

School. If his object were to see what the best of the higher religions have to offer intelligent, literate—*and desperate*—inquirers, he could now find it out with fewer transportation problems by reading Aldous Huxley's *Perennial Philosophy*.[21]

Huxley's impossible hope for a post-war international order based on a common recognition of a shared mystical philosophy dating back 2,500 years of course did not come to pass, nor did other hopes that the horrors of two World Wars would bring humanity to its senses. So the battlefield issues that Krishna and Arjuna address in the *Bhagavad Gita* and the complex teachings Krishna presents at Kurukshetra continue to find readers on modern battlefields. Let us take one last recent example.

Tulsi Gabbard, Democrat of Hawaii, was the first Hindu to be elected to the United States House of Representatives in 2012, and she decided to take her oath of office on a personal copy of the *Bhagavad Gita*. This work had offered great strength and reassurance to her, she explained to reporters, during her military deployment with the U. S. Army in Iraq. Serving in a field medical unit, surrounded by visible reminders of mortality, she gravitated to Krishna's teachings to Arjuna concerning the indestructibility of the soul. She quoted a favorite verse pertinent to her circumstances: "The soul can never be cut into pieces by any weapon, nor can it be burned by fire, nor moistened by water, nor withered by wind" (2.23). The *Gita*, she claimed, inspired her "to strive to be a servant-leader, dedicating my life in the service of others and to my country." Gabbard was one of the first two female combat veterans ever elected to Congress, and she continues to serve in the Army National Guard.

On fields of battle both literal and figurative, she surely will not be the last to have found inspiration from Krishna's teachings in the *Bhagavad Gita*.

Richard Davis

---

21. Emphasis mine. Signe Toksvig, *New York Times Book Review*, September 30, 1945, p. 3, in Donald Watt, *Aldous Huxley: The Critical Heritage* (London: Routledge & Kegan Paul, 1975), p. 361.

SUGGESTIONS FOR FURTHER READING

Mahabharata

The full *Mahabharata* is available in a complete translation by K. M. Ganguly, completed in 1896. More recent attempts to provide a full translation, not yet complete, are by J. A. B. Van Buitenen (1973–1978), James Fitzgerald and others (2004), published by University of Chicago Press; and by various translators through the Clay Sanskrit Series (2005–2009), published by New York University Press.

Several shorter publications convey portions of the immense riches of the great epic.

Narasimhan, Chakravarthi V. 1965. *The Mahabharata: An English Version Based on Selected Verses.* Records of Civilization, Sources and Studies 71. New York: Columbia University Press. Rev. ed. 1998.

> Prose telling, 216 pages. Narasimhan follows the order of the primary plot closely and provides an index of verses (about 4,000 verses out of the 100,000 in the original) on which the telling is based.

Satyamurti, Carole. 2015. *Mahabharata: A Modern Retelling.* New York: W. W. Norton.

> Retelling in blank verse, 843 pages. Fluent and largely faithful retelling, in iambic pentameter verse form, with some prose story insets. Lengthy, but an excellent representation that captures much of the plot and some of the didactic and narrative digressions.

Smith, John D. 2009. *The Mahabharata: An Abridged Translation.* Penguin Classics. London, New York: Penguin Books.

> Abridged translation, in prose. 791 pages, with sixty-page introduction. Aims at an accurate but digestible translation of portions of the original, focusing on the main plot. Translates about 11 percent of the original, with other portions summarized (in italics).

Bhagavad Gita (History, Translations, and Interpretations)

Davis, Richard H. *The Bhagavad Gita: A Biography.* Lives of Great Religious Books. Princeton: Princeton University Press, 2015.

Fitzgerald, James L. "The Great Epic of India as Religious Rhetoric: A Fresh Look at the Mahabharata." *Journal of the American Academy of Religion* 51, no. 4 (1983): 611–30.

Gandhi, Mohandas K. *The Bhagavad Gita According to Gandhi.* Berkeley, CA: Berkeley Hills Books, 2000.

Hijiya, James A. "The 'Gita' of J. Robert Oppenheimer." *Proceedings of the American Philosophical Society* 144, no. 2 (2000): 123–67.

Huxley, Aldous. *The Perennial Philosophy.* New York: Harper and Brothers, 1945.

Larson, Gerald James. "The Song Celestial: Two Centuries of the *Bhagavad Gita* in English." *Philosophy East and West* 31, no. 4 (1981): 513–41.

Minor, Robert N. *Bhagavad Gita: An Exegetical Commentary.* New Delhi: Heritage, 1982.

———. *Modern Indian Interpreters of the Bhagavadgita.* SUNY Series in Religious Studies. Albany: State University of New York Press, 1986.

Nagappa Gowda, K. *The Bhagavadgita in the Nationalist Discourse.* New Delhi: Oxford University Press, 2011.

Prabhavananda, Swami, and Christopher Isherwood. *The Song of God: Bhagavad-Gita.* Hollywood: Marcel Rood, 1944.

Sargeant, Winthrop. *The Bhagavad Gita.* SUNY Series in Cultural Perspectives. Albany: State University of New York Press, 2009.

Sharma, Arvind. *The Hindu Gita: Ancient and Classical Interpretations of the Bhagavad Gita.* LaSalle, IL: Open Court Publishing, 1986.

Zaehner, R. C. *The Bhagavad-Gita: With a Commentary Based on the Original Sources.* London: Oxford University Press, 1969.

GLOSSARY AND INDEX OF SANSKRIT NAMES AND TERMS

Adityas: The seven or twelve chief Hindu gods. 10.21, 11.22.

Agni: God of fire. 3.38, 10.23, 11.6.

ahamkara: Literally, "ego-making," having a concept of one's self. 13.8.

Airavata: Indra's elephant. 10.27.

Ananta: A serpent who symbolizes eternity. His name means "unending." 10.29.

Anantavijaya: Yudhishthira's conch shell. 1.16.

Arjuna: Hero of the *Bhagavad Gita*. One of the Pandavas, he is the son of Indra and Pritha or Kunti and the student of Krishna. 1.4, 1.15, 1.20, 1.24, 1.25, 1.26, 1.47, 2.1, 2.2, 2.4, 2.9, 2.10, 2.18, 2.32, 2.41, 2.42, 2.48, 2.54, 2.55, 2.68, 2.72, 3.1, 3.7, 3.19, 3.22, 3.36, 4.2, 4.4, 4.5, 4.34, 4.37, 5.1, 5.6, 6.16, 6.33, 6.37, 6.40, 6.43, 6.46, 7.7, 7.16, 7.26, 8.1, 8.4, 8.8, 8.14, 8.27, 9.3, 9.9, 9.13, 9.19, 9.23, 9.31, 10.12, 10.19, 10.24, 10.37, 10.39, 10.40, 10.42, 11.1, 11.6, 11.7, 11.13, 11.14, 11.33, 11.35, 11.47, 11.48, 11.50, 11.51, 11.54, 12.1, 12.7, 13.1, 13.26, 13.33, 14.3, 14.21, 15.19, 15.20, 16.3, 16.4, 16.5, 16.20, 17.1, 17.3, 17.26, 18.1, 18.4, 18.9, 18.13, 18.34, 18.35, 18.48, 18.50, 18.60, 18.61, 18.73, 18.76, 18.78.

Aryaman: The chief of the Pitris (ancestors of humanity). 10.29.

asat: Non-existence or unreality. The opposite of *sat*. 17.28.

Ashvatamma: Son of Drona and Kripa. One of the generals of the Kauravas. 1.8.

ashvatta: The sacred fig tree, also known as the pippala or bodhi. 15.1, 15.3.

Ashvins: Twin gods who ride in a chariot and usher in the dawn. 11.22.

Asita: A *rishi* (sage) to whom some of the hymns in the *Rig-Veda* are attributed. 10.13.

Asuras: A type of demon. 11.22.

Atman: The spiritual life principle of the universe. It is regarded as inherent in the individual self that transmigrates from one physical form to the next. 2.22, 3.17, 5.16, 5.18, 11.1, 14.5, 14.7, 14.20, 15.5, 15.11, 15.17.

Bhakti Yoga: The spiritual path of practicing devotion (*bhakti*) to a personal deity. 14.26.

Bharata: An ancient king of the Lunar Dynasty (Chandravansa). The name is also applied to his descendants, including Arjuna and Dhritarashtra. 2.10, 2.14, 2.30, 3.25, 3.41, 4.7, 4.42, 7.11, 7.27, 8.23, 14.8, 14.12, 18.4, 18.36, 18.62.

Bhima: One of the Pandavas. Son of Kunti and the wind god Vayu and half-brother of Arjuna. He is renowned for his great feats as a warrior. 1.4, 1.10, 1.15.

Bhishma: Son of the river goddess Ganga (the Ganges) who sides with the Kauravas in the war. 1.8, 1.10, 1.11, 1.25, 2.4, 11.26, 11.34.

Bhrigu: A *rishi* (sage) and one of the Prajapatis, who were the sons of Brahma and progenitors of humanity. 10.25.

Brahma: The creator of the universe. The first deity in the Trimurti (triad) with Vishnu and Shiva. 8.17, 8.18, 11.15, 11.37.

Brahman: The essential principle or spirit that underlies the entire universe; the cause of all existence. 2.46, 2.72, 3.15, 4.24, 4.25, 4.31, 4.32, 5.6, 5.10, 5.19, 5.20, 5.21, 5.24, 5.25, 5.26, 6.27, 6.28, 6.38, 7.29, 8.1, 8.3, 8.13, 8.16, 8.24, 10.12, 13.4, 13.12, 13.30, 14.3, 14.4, 14.26, 14.27, 17.23, 17.24, 18.50, 18.53, 18.54.

brahmin: A member of the priestly caste (the highest of the four castes). 5.18, 9.33, 17.23, 18.41, 18.42.

Brihaspati: A deity who acts as a priest, making sacrifices to the gods and aiding humanity by intervening with the gods. 10.24.

Brihatsaman: Hymns to Indra in the *Sama-Veda*, written in the thirty-six-syllable Brihati meter. 10.35.

Buddhi Yoga: The spiritual practice of using *buddhi*, the faculty of understanding and will, to apprehend *Atman* (the self). 10.10, 18.57.

Chekitana: An ally of the Pandavas. 1.5.

Chitraratha: Leader of the Gandharvas (celestial musicians). 10.26.

Devadatta: Arjuna's conch shell, given to him by Indra. 1.15.

Devala: A *rishi* (sage) to whom some of the hymns in the Vedas are attributed. 10.13.

dharma: Divine law; one's duty according to one's caste; righteous conduct. 4.7, 4.8, 11.18, 14.27.

Dhrishtadyumna: Son of Drupada and ally of the Pandavas. 1.17.

Dhrishtaketu: An ally of the Pandavas. 1.5.

Dhritarashtra: Blind Kuru king, son of Krishna Dvaipayana Vyasa and Arnbika, who supports his son Duryodhana and the Kauravas over the Pandavas. 1.1, 1.19, 1.20, 1.23, 1.24, 1.36, 1.37, 1.46, 2.6, 11.26.

dhyana: Meditation. 18.52.

Draupadi: Daughter of Drupada and wife of the Pandavas. 1.6, 1.18.

Drona: A Brahmin and the teacher of Duryodhana who sides with the Kauravas. Eventually he becomes the Kauravas' commander. 1.2, 1.8, 1.25, 2.4, 11.26, 11.34.

Drupada: Son of Prishata, father of Dhrishtadyumna, and father-in-law of the Pandavas. 1.3, 1.4, 1.18.

Duryodhana: Son of Dhritarashtra and Gandhari and leader of the Kaurava army. 1.2, 1.12, 1.23.

Gandharvas: Celestial musicians. 10.26, 11.22.

Gandiva: Arjuna's bow, given to him by the fire god Agni. 1.30.

Ganges: A sacred river in India, personified as a goddess. 10.31.

Garuda: King of the birds and bearer of Vishnu. 10.30.

Gayatri: A twenty-four-syllable meter used in the *Rig-Veda*. 10.35.

Govinda: "Cow finder," an epithet of Krishna. 1.32, 2.9.

gunas: The three basic constituent qualities of nature: *sattva* (goodness, luminosity, purity), *rajas* (passion, energy), and *tamas* (darkness, inertia). 2.45, 3.5, 3.27, 3.28, 3.29, 3.37, 4.13, 7.13, 7.14, 13.14, 13.19, 13.21, 13.23, 14.5, 14.18, 14.19, 14.20, 14.21, 14.23, 14.25, 14.26, 15.2, 15.10, 18.19, 18.29, 18.40, 18.41, 18.45.

Himalayas: A mountain range in central Asia whose name means "abode of snow." 10.25.

Ikshvaku: Son of Vaivasvata-Manu and founder of the Solar Dynasty (Suryavansa). 4.1.

Indra: God of the sky and father of Arjuna. 9.20, 11.6.

Janaka: A philosopher king who became a *Brahmin* (priest) and Rajarshi (royal sage). 3.20.

japa: Devotional repetition of a mantra or prayer. 10.25.

Jayadratha: A prince of the Lunar Dynasty (Chandravansa) and ally of the Kauravas. 11.34.

Jnana Yoga: *Jnana* means knowledge or wisdom. *Jnana Yoga* is the spiritual practice of using the mind to discover, or perceive directly, the nature of the self. 3.3.

kalpa: An enormously long period of time, an eon, an age of the universe, the exact length of which varies. 9.7.

Kama: God of love and desire. Also known as Kandarpa. 10.28.

Kamadhuk: A divine, wish-granting "cow of plenty." 10.28.

Kapila: A *rishi* (sage) who founded the philosophy of Samkhya. 10.26.

karma/karmic: Works or actions in and of themselves; also, the results of actions rebounding upon the doer. 2.39, 2.43, 4.19, 4.23, 5.2, 18.60.

Karma Yoga: Action *Yoga*, the spiritual practice of performing actions according to *dharma*, without attachment or regard to personal gain. 3.4, 5.2, 13.24.

Karna: Son of Pritha or Kunti and the sun god Surya. Although a half-brother to the Pandavas, he sides with the Kauravas out of gratitude to Duryodhana for making him king of Anga. 1.8, 11.26, 11.34.

Kashi: A country, most likely near modern Benares, whose king supports the Pandavas. 1.5, 1.17.

Keshin: A demon and enemy of the gods killed by Krishna. 18.1.

Krishna: An avatar of Vishnu, advisor to the Pandavas, and charioteer to Arjuna. 1.15, 1.21, 1.24, 1.28, 1.31, 1.36, 1.37, 1.39, 1.41, 1.44, 2.1, 2.9, 2.10, 2.54, 3.1, 3.36, 4.5, 5.1, 6.34, 6.35, 6.37, 6.38, 6.39, 6.40, 10.18, 11.2, 11.9, 11.35, 11.36, 11.41, 11.42, 11.50, 11.51, 13.1, 14.21, 17.1, 18.73, 18.74, 18.75, 18.76, 18.77.

kshatriya: A member of the caste of warriors and princes (the second of the four castes). 18.41, 18.43.

Kunti: Wife of Pandu and mother of Arjuna, Karna, and Yudhishthira, each by a different god. Also known as Pritha. 1.16, 1.27, 2.37, 2.60, 3.9, 5.22, 8.6, 8.16, 9.7, 9.10, 9.27, 14.4, 16.22.

Kuntibhoja: An ally of the Pandavas and adoptive father of Pritha or Kunti, mother of the Pandavas. 1.5.

Kurukshetra: "The field of Kuru," the plain on which the war recounted in the *Mahabharata* takes place. 1.1.

Kurus: A people who lived in the region of what is now Delhi. Also known as Kauravas. 1.12, 1.25.

Madhu: An evil *asura* (spirit) killed by Vishnu. 1.14, 1.35, 2.1, 8.2.

Manipushpaka: Sahadeva's conch shell. 1.16.

Manu: Founder of the human race. There are four of them, corresponding to the four ages of the world. 4.1, 10.6.

Marga-shirsha: A month that corresponds to parts of November and December. 10.35.

Marichi: One of the Prajapatis, who were the sons of Brahma and progenitors of humanity. He is a Marut, or storm god. 10.21.

Maruts: Storm gods and helpers of Indra. 10.21, 11.22.

Meru: The mountain on which the gods live. 10.23.

Nagas: A race of serpentine creatures. 10.29.

Nakula: One of the Pandavas. Son of Pandu's second wife Madri and one of the sky gods known as the Ashvins. Twin brother to Sahadeva. 1.16.

Narada: A *rishi* (sage) to whom some of the hymns in the *Rig-Veda* are attributed. 10.13, 10.26.

nirvana: A transcendent state of pure bliss, tranquility, and oneness with Brahman. Literally, the state of being blown out or extinguished. A term borrowed from Buddhism. One who attains nirvana is released from the cycle of death and rebirth. 2.72, 5.24, 5.25, 5.26, 6.15.

Om: A sacred syllable intoned during invocations, prayers, and meditation. 7.8, 8.13, 9.17, 10.25, 17.23, 17.24.

Om tat sat: A mantra. *Tat* means "this" or "that." *Sat* means truth, existence, reality. 17.23.

Panchajanya: Krishna's conch shell. It once belonged to a creature by the same name, whom Krishna killed. 1.15.

Pandavas: "Sons of Pandu": Yudhishthira, Bhima, Arjuna, Nakula, and Sahadeva. 1.3.

Pandu: Son of Krishna Dvaipayana Vyasa and Ambalika and father or stepfather of the Pandavas (Yudhishthira, Bhima, Arjuna, Nakula, and Sahadeva). He was the king of Hastinapura until he gave up the throne. 1.1, 1.2, 1.14, 1.20, 6.2, 10.37, 11.55, 14.22.

Paundra: Bhima's conch shell. 1.15.

Prahlada: A prince of the *daityas* (demons and enemies of the gods) who turned away from his race and became devoted to the worship of Vishnu. 10.30.

Prajapati: "Lord of Creatures." In the Vedas, this is the term used for the creator divinity; it later came to be applied to Brahma. 3.10.

prana: Vital energy; breath. 4.27.

pranayama: Breath control; a yogic meditation technique. 4.29.

Pritha: Wife of Pandu and mother of Arjuna, Karna, and Yudhishthira, each by a different god. Also known as Kunti. 1.25, 2.3, 2.21, 2.39, 3.16, 3.23, 4.11, 4.33, 6.1, 6.10, 8.22, 8.27, 11.5, 11.9, 12.7, 17.28, 18.6, 18.31, 18.32, 18.33, 18.72, 18.74.

Purujit: An ally of the Pandavas and brother of Kuntibhoja. 1.5.

rajas/rajasic: The *guna*, or quality, of passion and energy. 3.37, 7.12, 14.5, 14.7, 14.9, 14.10, 14.12, 14.15, 14.16, 14.17, 14.18, 17.1, 17.2, 17.4, 17.9, 17.12, 17.18, 17.21, 18.8, 18.21, 18.24, 18.27, 18.31, 18.34, 18.38.

Rakshas: A type of celestial spirit. 10.23.

Rama: There are three heroes with this name, but the one most often referred to is Ramachandra, hero of the *Ramayana*. He is an avatar of Vishnu, tasked with fighting the evil king Ravana. 10.31.

Rig-Veda: One of the four sacred texts known as the Vedas. 9.17.

rishi: A sage or seer. *Rishis* composed the Vedas. 4.2, 11.21.

Rudras: Gods of storms, destruction, and renewal, identified with the storm gods known as the Maruts. 10.23, 11.22.

Sadhyas: Celestial entities living in the ether. 11.22.

Sahadeva: One of the Pandavas. Son of Pandu's second wife Madri and one of the sky gods known as the Ashvins. Twin brother to Nakula. 1.16.

Sama-Veda: One of the four sacred texts known as the Vedas. 9.17, 10.22.

Samkhya: Literally, "reckoning" or "enumeration"; one of six Hindu schools of philosophy. Samkhya considers reality as bipartite: unchanging spirit (*purusha*) and ever-changing matter (*prakriti*). Samkhya divides material nature into twenty-five elements as well as recognizing the three *gunas* ("strands" or "constituents" of nature). 2.39, 3.3, 5.4, 5.5, 13.24, 18.13, 18.19.

samsara: The cycle of death and rebirth, entailing suffering, in the material world. 9.3.

Sanjaya: King Dhritarashtra's charioteer, bard, and ambassador who narrates most of the *Bhagavad Gita*. 1.1, 1.2, 2.1, 2.9, 11.9, 11.35, 18.74.

sat: "Reality" or "existence." It also carries the meanings "truth" and "goodness." 17.23, 17.26, 17.27.

sattva/sattvic: The *guna*, or quality, of goodness, luminosity, and purity. 7.12, 14.5, 14.6, 14.9, 14.10, 14.11, 14.14, 14.16, 14.17, 14.18, 17.1, 17.2, 17.4, 17.8, 17.11, 17.17, 17.20, 18.9, 18.20, 18.23, 18.26, 18.30, 18.33, 18.37.

Satyaki: An ally of the Pandavas. 1.17.

Shaibya: An ally of the Pandavas. 1.5.

Shankara: Another name for Shiva, the god of destruction and renewal and the second deity in the Trimurti (triad) with Brahma and Vishnu. 10.23.

Shikandi: Son of Drupada who kills Bhishma. He was a woman named Amba before his rebirth as a man. 1.17.

shudra: A member of the servant caste (the lowest of the four castes). 18.41, 18.44.

Skanda: The god of war, also known as Kartikeya. 10.24.

soma: The juice of a plant, whose identity is now unknown, used as a sacred drink in Vedic rituals. 9.20, 15.13.

Somadatta: Father of an ally of the Kauravas. 1.8.

Subhadra: Krishna's sister, Arjuna's wife, and the mother of his son Abhimanyu. 1.6, 1.18.

Sughosha: Nakula's conch shell. 1.16.

sutra: Sacred scripture. 13.4.

tamas/tamasic: The *guna*, or quality, of darkness and inertia. 7.12, 14.5, 14.8, 14.9, 14.10, 14.13, 14.15, 14.16, 14.17, 14.18, 16.22, 17.1, 17.2, 17.4, 17.10, 17.13, 17.19, 17.22, 18.7, 18.22, 18.25, 18.28, 18.32, 18.35, 18.39.

tat: "This" or "that." 17.23.

Ucchaishravas: Indra's horse. 10.27.

Ushana: An ancient seer. 10.37.

Ushmapas: "Steam Drinkers," a type of semi-divine ancestral being. 11.22.

Uttamaujas: An ally of the Pandavas. 1.6.

vaishya: A member of the caste of farmers and traders (the third of the four castes). 18.41, 18.44.

Vasava: Indra, especially in his role as the leader of the gods known as the Vasus. 10.22.

Vasudeva: Father of Krishna. 7.19, 10.37.

Vasuki: King of the Nagas (serpents). 10.28.

Vasus: A group of eight gods, led by Indra. The group consists of the gods of water, the pole-star, the moon, the earth, wind, fire, dawn, and light. 10.23, 11.22.

Vedanta: Literally, "the end (i.e., conclusion) of the Vedas," i.e., a school of religious thought based in the Upanishads. 15.15.

Vedas/Vedic: The four sacred Hindu texts (*Rig-Veda*, *Yajur-Veda*, *Sama-Veda*, and *Atharva-Veda*). The contents of the Vedas consist of both hymns and prose treatises. 2.42, 2.45, 2.46, 2.53, 4.28, 6.44, 7.8, 8.11, 8.28, 9.17, 9.20, 9.21, 10.22, 11.48, 11.53, 13.4, 15.1, 15.15, 15.18, 17.23, 17.24.

Vikarna: Brother of Duryodhana. One of the Kauravas. 1.8.

Virata: King of the district of Virata. He hosted the Pandavas during their exile and supports them in the war. 1.4, 1.17.

Vishnu: The preserver of the universe. The second deity in the Trimurti (triad) with Brahma and Shiva. 10.21, 11.24, 11.30.

Vishves: A group of twelve minor deities. 11.22.

Vittesha: "Lord of wealth," i.e., Kuvera, god of wealth. 10.23.

Vivasvat: God of the sun. 4.1, 4.4.

Vrishni: A member of the Yadava lineage, of which Krishna is the last member. 10.37.

Vyasa: A sage to whom the compilation of the Vedas is attributed. He is the father of Pandu and grandfather of the Pandavas. 10.13, 10.37, 18.75.

Yadu: Ancestor of the Yadava branch of the Lunar Dynasty (Chandravansa), of which Krishna is the last member. 11.41

Yajur-Veda: One of the four sacred texts known as the Vedas. 9.17.

Yakshas: A type of celestial spirit. 10.23, 11.22.

Yama: God of death and the Underworld. 10.29.

Yoga/yogic: Literally, "union" or "joining" (cognate with English "yoke"); one of six major Hindu schools of philosophy. As a meditation practice *Yoga* seeks "union" with one's own essence and therefore with the essence of the universe. 2.39, 2.48, 2.50, 2.53, 2.61, 3.3, 3.7, 4.1, 4.2, 4.3, 4.27, 4.28, 4.38, 4.41, 4.42, 5.1, 5.2, 5.4, 5.5, 5.6, 5.7, 5.21, 6.2, 6.3, 6.4, 6.12, 6.16, 6.17, 6.19, 6.20, 6.23, 6.28, 6.29, 6.33, 6.36, 6.37, 6.41, 6.44, 7.1, 7.25, 8.8, 8.10, 8.12, 8.27, 9.5, 9.22, 9.28, 10.7, 10.10, 10.18, 11.4, 11.9, 11.47, 12.1, 12.6, 12.9, 12.11, 13.10, 13.24, 14.26, 16.1, 18.33, 18.52, 18.57, 18.75, 18.78.

yogin: One who practices *Yoga* and achieves integration with the self and therefore with all beings. 3.3, 4.18, 4.25, 5.5, 5.8, 5.11, 5.12, 5.24, 6.1, 6.2, 6.8, 6.10, 6.15, 6.18, 6.19, 6.27, 6.28, 6.31, 6.32, 6.42, 6.45, 6.46, 6.47, 8.14, 8.23, 8.25, 8.27, 8.28, 10.17, 12.14.

Yudhamanyu: An ally of the Pandavas. 1.6.

Yudhishthira: Son of Kunti or Pritha and Dharma. The eldest Pandava, he is the just and virtuous king of Indraprastha. 1.16.

yuga: An age, especially one of the four ages of the world in Hindu chronology. 8.17.

Yuyudhana: An ally of the Pandavas. 1.4.